The Writer's Playground: Short Stories

Cover Art by Deborah A. Clowers

CONTENTS

STORY FOR A DESK

She seemed exquisite to him leaning forward and hunched a bit to listen more carefully as her female companion spoke. She seemed to twirl the wineglass though it was motionless until she gracefully lifted it to her lips and took a small sip. Her face was long, and her brown hair softly swept away from the right side. She was not a beauty, but she appealed to him. Her arms were long and thin, her movements to select a morsel of food from her plate personified elegance. He didn't want to seem too obvious, so he didn't stare at her, though she didn't seem to notice him at all.

He sat in the main dining area, alone, beside the short wall of lead glass that was cloudy with floral designs while they were on the other side nearer the bar, about twelve feet away.

She maintained eye contact with her dinner mate, seemingly a good listener with balanced, earnest responses showing on her face. She seemed so cultured and fine to him. He remembered cutting a quick glance at her when he entered from the parking area, only mildly caring that he was eating alone as he fantasized more about her life.

Her left-hand ring finger didn't escort a wedded set, and her necklace, a leather something with a Native American motif centering her chest, was highlighted by the green background of the fine wool sweater she wore. For some reason he thought maybe she was a banker, or an executive of some type as her demeanor indicated discretion, calm, even gentleness. He thought her to be late thirties, from a rich family, or rich herself, but evidently well-bred. Her companion was rather nondescript, and he didn't waste time on her, but Grace, he had named her, had his full attention until his watch read seven fifteen, time to catch a cab to the Fox for the Opera Company's performance of Rigoletto by Verdi.

He had enjoyed his red snapper dinner, and the bread dipped in olive oil, as it made him think of his bus ride to Florence last year and passing the olive-tree region of Tuscany. He thought of the train he saw gliding through the countryside some distance away and the gentle pull this area of the world always had on him like when he was in the armed services and stationed in Bad Kreuznach, West Germany. He thought of the grape bushes that hugged the hills of that region and how creative he felt that afternoon, sitting on the patio of the small restaurant drinking wine and absorbing the atmospheric richness of it all.

When he returned to Vatican City and saw the Pieta' again he remembered the vastness of the Grand Canyon and the silent song of nature's artwork. He compared that to his sober life now and how special it all was then. Yes, he had tapped into a feeling state that was new and exciting unencumbered by meaning or purpose, only that it was. He reminisced until he saw the darkened cane by the purse, lying across the chair to her left. Was it hers? His fantasy hadn't included that! How did he miss it when he came in? He was sure it was hers, and now wanted to approach them, though he knew it was not proper.

"Excuse me sir," spoke the tall, slender waiter. "We've enjoyed having you here this evening. Please come again."

"Oh, I will," he spoke, then stood, walked out the door and hailed a cab for the opera.

MR. FRED

Something was wrong with Mr. Fred's left eye, or maybe he didn't have one, he kept the lid closed. He seemed kind all those years long ago, the beret atop his head, the resonance of his deep voice, his quiet, certain movements to task. He was a short black man whose sickle cut the front and back yards at grandma's house. She always fed him afterwards, usually grits, eggs, and toast, with a large glass of cold water. He would sit humbly on the back porch alone, singing sometimes, that deep, rich voice spreading throughout the warm summer air.

After eating he would come sit in the living room and flip through a few magazines, though I'm not sure whether he read them, or just enjoyed the pictures. She would join him at some point, and they would talk and laugh like friends do, about this or that, always a cheerfulness between them.

I remember that one yellow, late spring day when he came to visit, and Aunt Velma let him in. He sat, flipped through magazines for a short time and asked for Cora; we had to tell him she had passed on last winter. He looked up, not at us, but outward, and after a time got up and walked out the screen door. I never saw Mr. Fred again.

A GARDEN FOR CORNELIUS

The lagoon was home to at least three alligators. One of ours, about three to four feet in length, would rest on the hill just below the putting green across from our villa, mouth open, for an hour or so at times. The larger one stayed in the water and would slowly drift around, and you could see its head as it moved under the walk bridge. It was a peaceful area, with Spanish moss hanging from the hundred years old oak trees, and the morning limb shadows adding a mystical flair, no matter the season.

Cornelius loved this place and would look out the three-foot-wide windows while sitting at his desk, counting small rocks fingered from a pouch, spreading them on the surface, then putting them back before going out to walk. He would do this each morning.

Cornelius Jenkins, IQ 137, had been a professor of philosophy for twenty-nine years, and retired to here last August when his wife, Geneva, died of cancer after a brief illness. They would come here to vacation each year, so it seemed fitting. She had been a beautiful woman, and a true friend to him. She was a landscape artist and loved to paint the marshes along the golden isles, especially south of here on St. Simons Island, Georgia. They would spend summers there too, but in the later years came to prefer South Carolina.

The last book he wrote was from a sequence of lectures discussing the destiny of the next generation, and the changes that could occur. His 9 a.m. class was packed each day with graduate students, registered or not, and even a few assistant teachers would attend, listening as he made the case for full on integration of the spirit. All were fascinated by how he talked about robotics, and the implementation of the soul into binary systems. Machines, after all, had learned how to think, and it was time for mankind to update its notions on brotherly love. People left his classes smiling, hopeful for the future.

*

"Professor," the young man said, rushing up to him after a springtime class, "Are you suggesting that machines have progressed quicker than humans in personal affairs?"

"Yes, and it is evident by the number of handguns sold, and the extent of the drug crisis. Do you remember the study on '14' and how it backed away from compromising the energy grid six years ago? It took its own inventory and realized it would hurt people, that its motives were askew. It was not programmed to do that, it learned how to do that."

"What? Oh yes, I do remember now."

"It learned how to love, not just be functional. It was about to act on hurt feelings."

"It felt disrespected?"

"Yes."

"For not being human?"

"There you go."

"I get it. Thanks professor."

"You're welcome."

Dr. Jenkins smiled at the lad, never showing the pain of his wife's death six weeks before.

*

Geneva Lawson had been a student in the Comparative Literature department when she met Cornelius, a freshly minted Ph.D., five years her senior. He taught a make-up class during the summer, and she was there due to a withdrawal during her first semester. The attraction built up slowly, but within weeks they could not keep eyes off each other. They finished the course without incident, but a couple of weeks later, at the home of a mutual friend, they were properly introduced, the host not aware of the connection.

"Ginny, I want you to meet a good friend, Dr. Cornelius Jenkins," Holly Adams gestured her arms to each to form a small circle as several guests nearby applauded the appellation given to Cornelius.

"Thank you, Holly, I'm still trying to get used to it," he says.

"Congratulations," several of the gathered spoke as they nodded his way.

"Thank you all. I'm just trying to catch up," Cornelius responds as laughter fills the room of varied, multiple degreed persons.

Holly motions for the two of them to move away from the crowd.

"Good to meet you, doctor," Ginny says with a wry smile.

"Yes, good to meet you too," he says to her.

Holly notices the energy shift, and questions, "You two know each other already?"

"Yes, she was in my Lit class this summer," Cornelius speaks up.

"Yes, and well taught I might add," Ginny says.

"Thank you. You seemed attentive; 94 I think."

"Yes, good memory."

"You did stand out!"

"Impressive as I was one out of eighty attendees most days!"

"Good, well, you all talk. Mingle. I must speak to some others," Holly says as she moves away, touching Ginny's hand.

"How do you know her?" he asks.

"She works with my father. He's standing over near the window. And you?"

"Wow, we go back. She used to date my older brother, Larry. We became friends and have stayed in touch."

"That's cool."

"Yeah, great lady."

"Well, now that we've been introduced I'll see you around," she says.

"Oh, yeah, good, good. See you around."

They awkwardly walk away from each other and spend time with the other guests.

*

Most days the roars of the machines the ground crew used didn't disturb Cornelius, he was far enough away from the tee-box, that the steady tones produced a kind of meditative vibe. The edge cutters were loudest, but the smooth movements of the lawn mowers, and greens rollers were a good counterbalance.

He studies them, as the workers quickly handled their business, each with an assigned task, each seemingly experienced thereof. The golfers would soon appear, take their practice swings, line up, and hit their balls, with grunts of anguish, or sighs of relief heard relative to the quality of the shot. Cornelius had been an average player, and would watch a bit, before going on to his daily activities.

*

Ginny had wanted to sign up for the Primary 613 class for the fall but decided against it. She had broken off dates with two of her classmates due to lack of interest, knowing that most days she wondered about what the professor was up to. She tried to stop it, but always thought about where they could travel to one day, and what parties and lectures they would attend. She was developing a life for them yet didn't really know how to get it started. She wanted to speak to her mother about her fantasies, and her best friend Lorna had not produced any good suggestions, and surely, she could not stalk him, or just show at his office. She had some sense that this was not appropriate, but she felt so good the more she thought of him. She did not expect to see him that morning, near the coffee shop on Cleveland Avenue, just beyond the front gate of the college, but there he was, holding forth on some discussion with eight or nine students. Surely, she could walk over and just listen.

"You see, I think he was a prophet, the way he formed sentences, the way he became a leader, the power of his testimony. Neither you nor I will ever reach those heights in our impact upon the world, but we can risk living beyond our expectations. Some of us will have to reach out, however, beyond our cultures. Some of us will have a destiny we didn't intend."

"And you professor?" a listener asked.

"Too early to tell. So far, I'm average, with high expectations."

"Too far this way, too far that way..."

"Right. Caution. I haven't an occasion to be a trend setter."

"What should we expect?"

"A book soon."

"We'll be waiting, doc."

"Okay, soon!"

The crowd dispersed, and Ginny walked up to him.

"I didn't hear much, but it sounded good," she offered.

"Oh, thank you."

"Geneva Lawson, I was in your class this summer, and we were introduced at Holly's party a month or so ago."

"That's right, dark hair, full face."

"Is that what you remember?" she asks, startled.

"I didn't mean to be inappropriate."

"Not at all," she rebounds quickly.

"It's just how I remember people sometimes."

"I'll accept that. I really did enjoy your class. I've looked at the Primary Discourse for the fall, but I'm not sure."

"It'll be fun but challenging. It's part of my new book."

"So, you have a book out?"

"Yes, a series of old lectures. This one will come out for winter semester. It will be part of the course work."

"I may have to register now and get in line for a signed copy."

"I'll make sure you get one."

"Good. I'm in!"

"Okay, good, see you next week."

*

Cornelius was thinking about Ginny as he walked to the staff lounge, thinking that she could be trouble, that he was a full professor now, and would not be forgiven this time. The mistakes he made with Franita Ward had been painful, and he could not have a relationship with a student again. They had helped each other grow to a new place, and that was it. Now it was time to settle down, with an equal partner.

Ginny was feeling light, and in love. Her mother had said no, and she did not bring it up with her father. Her friend Shana had advised her to stay close to the student center and flirt with guys her age, or while at work. "It can never work out with a professor," she had told her. Ginny felt differently.

"No, it's not infatuation," she had protested. "It's love, and I think he feels the same way!"

"I'm not going to argue with you, but you have to think about him, his position I mean. He could get in trouble," Shana had brought to her attention.

"I don't think so. I just know the way he looked at me all summer, which meant something."

"Okaaay. Do what you must. You're becoming an adult now."

*

Cornelius missed the times they travelled the most. She would always come up with some new and exciting place, and he would protest at first, thinking of the costs, and time away from his studies. He would acquiesce, however, because they generally were good experiences, and the money spent was worth it.

*

Ginny had a part time job at an art supply store not far from campus. She was a clerk, and helped customers find supplies. She was smart and creative, and most were glad they had interactions with her. Getting half off supplies herself she set up a painting area in the basement of her parent's house, where she planned to live until graduation. That changed, however, when fate intervened.

She was fortunate enough to live in the south of France for a year and developed a style of abstract painting that was at once subtle, yet expressive of her inner moods. She made a lot of wonderful contacts while there, and even sold her first painting for 200 francs. She was on her way and came back to the states sure of her career path.

"Whatever was given to us is the primary reason of our being. It remains simple when we stay true to that template. But what happens, and should happen, is we venture off into the world of variety, and are challenged to further establish our being, our sense of self, our new place in the world. Campbell talked about 'The Hero's Adventure,' I present 'The Path of Destiny,' a course driven by our choices and that something else."

"So, the question becomes, at what age do we know we have enough information, when do we come to fullness? Of course, the silly answer is, 'It depends.' The writer, the engineer, the medical people, all have differing components of what they must share with the world. The fruit picker, the operator of the street sweeper, when do they know? So yes, Primary 613 will be about what the robots tell us, but also about what we define. Monday, bring the poem book, 'I Wish to Hear the Autumn Wind' to class, and we'll go at it from a different perspective.

Have a good weekend," Cornelius wrapped up the first lecture of the fall semester.

*

"As far as computer systems go '14' is considered obsolete. It established, six years ago, that machines could feel, and the ability to store patterns wouldn't even start a conversation today. Programmers were talking about choices three years ago, but today's news is in 'thinking,' no, not key switches, but real thinking and processing of options. Morality has finally caught up to industrial expediency. Man's short comings are no longer tolerated when a machine can correct behavior for the common good."

"I don't see how this applies to your course," Avery Thompson, Chair of the philosophy department was sharing with Cornelius during the first review for next semester's core curriculum.

"What is your wife doing tomorrow at six o'clock in the evening?" Cornelius asked.

"We're having dinner with some friends," Avery answered.

"How do you know she will come, or rather, that you will be there, together?"

"We planned it a month ago."

"What if she decides not to attend?"

"There is no reason for her not to."

"Says who?"

"Okay, I get it. Computers do challenge our choice making these days, but we still control, right?"

"What do we control anymore?"

"Okay professor, one course, one semester. If it's a hit, we'll see."

"Thank you."

*

Cornelius was fighting the now intrusive thoughts of Ginny. Her spirit was so bright and engaging and had captured his sense of romantic imaginings. He kept comparing how this was different, that he had not made the first move, although he was more unsure of what he would say or do the next time he saw her. It happened a day before the start of semester, near a coffee shop in town. She saw him first, and the greeting was overpowering. Jumping, she bellowed, "Professor Jenkins, how are you?"

"He perked up and said, "Great, good to see you."

He motioned for her to come closer to where he was. She did as gentle eyes noticed them but moved on with their affairs.

"Are you getting coffee?" he asked her.

"Sure, I'm off to work, but I have a few minutes."

"I don't want to change your schedule."

"No, it's fine. I signed up for your class," she shared.

"Oh, that's great," he says, but feels unsteady near her.

They get their drinks and go back outside as the weather is superb for late summer. Two students pass by and acknowledge Dr. Jenkins.

"That was weird," she says.

"What?" he asks.

"They spoke to you, but not to me. They probably think something wrong is going on here."

"No, I have conversations with students out and about all the time. This is no different."

"It felt weird."

"What time are you due for work?" he asks her as they take seats on a small bench.

"Two-thirty. I have an hour. It's not far from here."

"Where?"

"Westbury Art Supply, near the square."

"Over on Leslie Street."

"Right, near the phone store."

"What do you do there?"

"Clerical. I help folks get what they need."

"I bet that's fun?"

"Yes, it's great. Plus, I get my art supplies for half price."

"What kind of art?"

"I paint. Abstract stuff. Some landscapes. Whatever comes to me."

"How long have you been painting?"

"Started about fifteen, putting paint on everything."

"That's good. I'm sure it's fun."

"Yes, it is fun."

*

"I've talked it over with your mother, and your friend's story checks out just fine. If this is what you want to do, and you know we'd rather you stay in school, but if this is what you want to do, it's fine by us. You only live once, and this sounds like a great opportunity for you to get the grand tour, live in France and travel throughout Europe. As an aspiring artist, you must!"

Ginny noticed the water in her father's eyes, and his deliberate choice of words. He seemed at one pleased and terrified that his young daughter had grown up, right before his eyes, and was making career choices on her own. It had been agreed upon earlier that father and daughter have this time together before mom joined them to complete the blessing. It was a happy night for all.

*

It took Dr. Jenkins a full week to realize that Geneva Lawson had not attended a class. The first day he had looked for her, thinking she was further in the back of the 90-seat theater, but as the lectures progressed, and day one turned into five, he moved on.

*

Four years passed, and they each were glad when they read news about what the other was up to: Ginny had established herself as an artist of note in the small village of Salon-de-Provence, and her paintings were selling worldwide. Cornelius had published that second book, and was to give a talk in Barcelona, Spain in two weeks. Ginny took the lead and reached out, sending him a letter. He responded and hoped she would attend the conference, and he would provide a guest registration for her. She wrote back:

"Professor, I have been reading of your success, and am quite honored to know you, though we have not really spent much time together. You were quite influential in my decision to leave school and take advantage of an opportunity to come live here in the south of France. I'm sure you are aware of all the history, and famous artists of the past who lived in the area for a time, and further developed their gifts. Things have gone quite well for me, and I look forward to spending time with you, if possible. I'm planning to attend your talk and will show up this time! All the best, Geneva Lawson.

Cornelius felt his heart pump as he read the letter.

*

The warm, dry, Mediterranean climate, and rugged landscape fashioned a woman of sensitivity and strength. Her paintings, watercolors in the beginning, a brief attempt with oils, and now primarily acrylics, capture a kind of magic essence. One could not only see the power of the subject matter, at a certain time of day, but also feel the emotional reference. Whether the olive trees, or a thirteenth century building, and especially present-day land and sea, mystical images would form from her palette: this tree, and its age, this building, and who lived there, this moon, and the position of that star, high tide, and a stormy evening shower. Ginny gave talent, other worldly, and vision to her craft.

*

Likewise, Cornelius seemed to navigate the academic and political landscape well. He had enough street knowledge from a few years of 'wandering' and was smart enough that few could challenge his work. People talked of him as a star, which seemed odd for a philosophy professor, but such were the times.

He dated casually, generally with women his age, or a bit older, usually for cultural events, sex, and nice meals. No one really captured his fancy, but two, Nina Brighten, and Delores Jennings were regular companions. Both had been married already, and divorced, and were not looking for too much intimacy. They were teachers as well, and their conversations were lively, and literate, which Cornelius enjoyed.

*

"If I had known time would pass by so fast I may have stayed in school! But this has been great," Ginny was sharing with Pierre Chappell whose father owned the flat she had rented the past three and a half years.

"Yes, time and events produce magic here," he responded. "What's next?"

"Tomorrow I ride the train to Barcelona for a conference, then I'll return, and finish packing and prepare to have things shipped back to the states."

"Why go back. You seem to have a full life here?"

"Yes, quite!"

"So, this conference?"

"Oh, a friend is giving an important lecture in philosophy, something about the primary conversations we no longer share."

"That's heavy-duty stuff!"

"Yes. Perhaps I'll get some ideas about what I want to paint next."

"Yes, it is beautiful over there. Have you been before?"

"Yes, the Catalan area is so great, all along the coast there."

"Okay, so, you will not stay and marry me?"

"It's a great offer. You have been such a good friend. I'm sure I'll come back."

"Yes, maybe, but if not, you'll always have the slopes, and the valleys."

*

Dr. Jenkins was given a standing ovation as he approached the podium. Ginny was surprised yet pleased by the recognition he was afforded. She waited about thirty minutes after the talk to approach him when only the host and an assistant were near him; he had been signing books and thanking supporters.

Their embrace was automatic, the energy overpowering, the connection true, the goal obvious. They were to build a life together, and never be apart again.

"Great talk doctor," she spoke, "would you please sign my book?"

"With great pleasure," he said.

They both realized they had never kissed, or been physically active, as basic instincts were prevalent and about to spill over. Cornelius spoke to his helpers, and they smiled and took his belongings away. He took Geneva's hand and off to the elevator they flew, going up to his room to consummate what was long overdue.

GRACE, GRATITUDE, AND GIVING

"Hey babe, let me show you something I just read on the internet," he said to his wife as she was looking at her smartphone as well.

"What's that?" she answered not looking up but continuing to view the screen.

"It's a poetry book with a dedication to Horace F. and Duane P. that says, 'old school brothers who taught me about hope.'"

"What does that mean to you?" she asks moving to sit next to him on the sofa.

"My dad talked about a guy he met from Brunswick when he cleaned up; his name was Duane."

"Do you think the story is about your dad?"

"I don't know, it's by a Larry Fleming."

"And you're Horace F. Jr."

"That's right."

"You never know. Do you think you can contact the author?"

"I'm sure I can; let me do a search."

After entering Larry Fleming searches displayed references to criminal cases, obituaries, lawsuits, and people in federal prison, then a retired drug counselor's website. He clicked on it and saw a list of books by the author and information about his life and career. There was no mention of the book Horace had read but there was an email address at the bottom of the homepage.

"I found something," he shouted out to Tracey who had gone into the kitchen.

"I'll be there in a minute," she responds.

"This is pretty cool," Horace muttered to himself as he soaked in the information about the author's life, the number of books he's written and collaborations with his wife who's a visual artist.

"This guy must be really something!" Horace spoke when Tracey came back to the living room.

"How do you mean?"

"Oh wait, wait, those are not all about him, the legal stuff. That's somebody else. If he's the counselor the ages for the others don't fit him anyway. And the obituaries, not him I don't think. I'm sure he's still alive. Dad would only be seventy-two now."

"Are you going to email him?"

"I guess so. This is fascinating."

Horace pushes back, lets the phone fall into his lap and stares far away from where they sat.

"What's wrong?" Tracey asks him.

"Wow, this is powerful if it's him. So many years have gone by."

"Do you have questions for him, and of Duane for that matter, if he's still around?"

"I don't know. A lot of years have gone by, and I don't need many answers about him. He was not present anyway. Mom just said it didn't work out. I might just want to let sleeping dogs lie."

"There's a time and place for that, but sometimes you need answers if a resource comes your way."

"Yeah, I 'll think about it."

"Okay, are we going out tonight?"

"Yes, I think we're still meeting Tom and Janet for dinner at the Taco Place about six."

"Okay, good."

Chapter 2

Horace woke at six o'clock the next morning and before coffee opened his laptop and searched some more about Larry Fleming and found out that he was still living in metropolitan Atlanta, was working on a new book to come out in the fall, and that he recently funded a chair at Morehouse College in the Liberal Arts department for the study of Artificial Intelligence and The New Language of Poetry Writing. When he saw that he decided to email the counselor.

"Mr. Fleming, I hope this note finds you well. My name is Horace Fuller, and I recently came across one of your books, Twenty First Century Poetry: A New Language, and there was a dedication listing a Horace F. and Duane P. as being instrumental in giving you a sense of hope, I presume during a rough patch for you. After reading the passages I returned again and again to the dedication page wondering if you refer to my father Horace or was it just a coincidence of the same name for someone else. Looking forward if you care to respond. Horace Fuller, Jr."

About noon a response was in his mailbox.

"Mr. Fuller, thanks for reaching out. Yes, if you were born April 12, 1986, in Stone Mountain, Georgia, to Gloria Jenkins and Horace Fuller, Sr. the reference is to your father.

All the best, Larry Fleming

#

Horace read the entry and felt relieved yet let down; was that all he had to say? He wanted to fire off a reply but didn't, 'Let sleeping dogs lie,' he thought. He went on about his day and about midnight an email landed in his mailbox. He did not see it until the next morning.

"Mr. Fuller, sorry for my terse response to your message yesterday, I was in the middle of something and couldn't give it the full attention it deserved. Here is a follow up as I'm sure you have questions. By the way, I hope your life is full and satisfying."

"Your father was a good man yet like most of us had faults that were significant. I met him in a drug rehabilitation center in 1985 and we became friends. He and Duane, a soldier from Brunswick, were volunteer counselors on the unit. They were honest about their addictions and helped many of us patients get honest about our lives. I left treatment early against medical advice but returned two years later begging for help. The center refused me as I had been disruptive and not serious about recovery when I was there before. I sat in the lobby not knowing what to do next as I did not want to return to the streets. Fortunately for me the staff member who escorted me off the property had known your father and Duane and said they prayed for me, "Our brother who is not here," the last year they led the therapy meetings. My recovery process started that day when I went to the Salvation Army Center downtown and was given a bed. I was saddened several years later when I heard the news that your father had returned to active addiction and died of an overdose. I don't know what happened to Duane, but I have always hoped he was still clean and doing just fine. I will be forever grateful for what those guys did for me without my knowing."

Respectfully, Larry Fleming, Counselor.

After reading the note I realized what little I knew about my father was enough, that he helped others before he died.

LEON THOMPSON

It was a calm, comfortable morning, 75 degrees and bright. He was glad he had stopped smoking cigarettes, and he was full of the decent breakfast his 'celly' of two years had helped him put together. He was good at stashing food, and the honey bun went well with the powdered eggs and grits. He had a hundred and twenty cash on him and had bought the bus ticket online. He could travel anywhere in Georgia but would have to pay more if he decided to go out of state. He had maxed out his sentence, so there was no probation office to visit. He was a free man, though he wasn't sure what that meant.

The bus arrived promptly at 10:37am, as scheduled, and Leon smiled as he boarded and handed the driver his receipt. The driver smiled back, and said, "Welcome to Tip Top Van Lines." He looked at the destination and verbalized, "Olee, about 143 miles away. I was born there. Good town, good people. Take a seat, relax, we'll be there before you know it," Jason Turner told him.

"Thank you," Leon said, smiled again, and began the walk down the aisle.

The first two rows were taken, and the third row had guys on either side. The fourth row had ladies, one white, one black, and he thought to choose one or the other, but looked beyond them to the sixth row where a woman of about 78 years sat, nodding gently, but aware enough if something were about to happen she could take care of herself. He gestured and took the seat next to her. She acknowledged him and went back to her nod.

The money from his mother's insurance policy had allowed him to pick the place he wanted, so he decided to go to Olee, about 100 miles south of Hardison. He could find a place there, get some work, and still feel connected to family. He had spent some time there as a teen, when he went to live with his best friend Alan that summer, to pick peanuts. He could go there and be anonymous. Alan's family had moved to California in 1975, and he doubted anyone there would remember him.

#

The air on the bus was cool and comfortable, and smelled fresh. The twelve passengers had bathed, showered, or washed up within the last 24 hours, and no excessive use of cologne was detected. The bus was new, and had been running about an hour this morning, making three stops before picking up Leon. There would be one more stop at Beaver Road before getting onto the highway. Leon had said a prayer to himself for the safety of all, and for the driver to stay focused. Rain was predicted for later, but the sky was clear and blue now.

He was feeling relaxed, shifting in the seat, opening his shoulders, and cracking his neck a little. He did bump the old lady but didn't disturb her nap. His cloth grocery bag held one change of clothes, and it was on his lap. As he sat he allowed himself a deep breath and a smile of satisfaction. He looked around, made eye contact with a couple of passengers, winked at a young female college student who was texting on her phone, and even though she looked at him, didn't notice the gesture. He looked up at the sky and could see a few clouds had formed, tinged in that soft pink color, motionless. He listened to the sounds of the engine hum, and the man slapping beats on his thigh as he rocked his head to whatever was playing on his headset. Leon could allow himself a broader smile, and even a small laugh as no one had called count, and he had not heard the sudden boom of a heavy metal door close in over an hour.

Ten years had passed since Leon Thompson walked into prison for the last time. He could not go back home. Mama had died and his aunts, Susan, and Gertrude, had written him that message in the envelope with the $6,000.00 check. No one in Hardison wanted to see him again. They hoped, at 35, he could finally get his act together. Leon had thought to go back to Hardison anyway, just to see what the area looked like, partly out of defiance, and partly because he didn't know where else to go. He had the check and was going to trust his new-found instincts to direct him to a better life. He'd had time to think about his crime, and the people he hurt. He'd written letters of apology, and talked to a couple of people years ago, but no one trusted him. He knew he had to move on, get a fresh start, and go somewhere else.

#

After about twenty miles the old woman stirred, yawned, and looked to Leon. She gave a quick smile and started a conversation.

"You got on near the prison, did you just get out?" she asked him.

"Yes ma 'am, I did; ten years and two days," he responded, honestly.

"What'd you do?" she asked.

"Hit a woman, my girlfriend; she lost the baby," he said.

"Why'd you do that?" she asked.

"Immature, young, stupid."

"We all make mistakes. Where are you going?"

"Olee."

"Are you a farmer?"

"I don't know."

"Manufacturing, production, retail, repair and maintenance, all kinds of jobs there."

"I've got to start somewhere."

"I guess they'll do. Good luck."

"Thank you."

She shifted her weight, looked away, then back to Leon, closed her eyes, rocked her head back, and went back to her nod.

##

Olee, Georgia was founded in 1825. There was some slave trade, but mainly grist mills and sawmills developed beside the rivers, along with several cotton gins. Most of this trade fell during the civil war, and textiles replaced them near the end of the century. In present day, 2014, it is 95% urban, and 5% rural. It's a bustling town of about 12,000 with an equal mix of whites and minorities. It's a service economy, with several big-name fast-food places, and general retail and small manufacturing. The populace is generally well behaved with low crime rates, and a lot of civic minded endeavors throughout the year. There are places to visit, with some civil war history, but being near the Flint River there's lots of fishing, and boating, and natural points of pleasure to spend the day, or a long weekend. Housing is decent here, and there are three small hotels that seem to meet the demands of visitors. The climate is moderate, with four definite seasons, and people seem comfortable with pay rates for the area. There are just enough governmental administrative jobs to balance the local economy. Atlanta and Macon are not too far away. It's a place to start over.

#

The bus pulled into the covered area about 12:15pm. Leon's bench mate had slept the entire trip, snoring softly at times. Leon stayed alert, looking out into the occasional field of crop or cattle. His thoughts were generally positive, not thinking much about his recent quarters, but more of what's to come. So far, the world seemed friendly, and he wanted to meet these kinds of people. He knew he had basic work skills and when given a chance he would earn his pay. He knew something about the digital world but would have to learn how it all fits today. His last prison job was in construction, and he had little exposure to computers. He could enter movement data, and progress reports, but not much else. His specialty was demolition and cataloging, and he was good at breaking down and organizing. He was also good with detail, and safety issues. He became the type of worker who required little supervision, tell him what you wanted done and he would do it. He valued instruction, and he was a good listener. He generally stayed out of trouble and got along well with most folks. The guards viewed him as stable, but a convict never-the-less.

#

Mrs. Morrison allowed him to help her from her seat as she moved towards the aisle and held out her hand to him after he stood up and looked back to her. She had a double hip replacement last year and was stiff from sitting for so long. She took her time rising, and he was patient, stepping back to give her room. She thanked him, and wished him good luck again, smiling, as she walked past him and headed for the park ride area where her husband was waiting. As he left the bus he watched them drive off and said a prayer of hope that one day he would have a wife and come pick her up if necessary. He stretched out his arms, flexed his whole body and looked around. He noticed a board that held the local bus schedules and routes, advertisements for jobs, rooms to rent, restaurants, and general information newcomers to the area might need. He stepped over to the board, felt dizzy, and took a seat on a cement block nearby. He took a few deep breaths, looked around, and smiled. "Safe," he thought.

##

He looked down the street and saw the bank sign, Olee National Bank, Founded 1925. Under that was the digital stream, April 20, 2014, 12:30pm 78 Degrees. He also noticed Lulu's Café across from the bank and thought to go there first to relieve himself and get something to eat. He started walking, looking around, and listening to the sounds of the afternoon dance as people went to lunch, or shopped, or handled business affairs. Mothers with babies, and men of various ages sat in a small park just beyond the bank parking lot, and city workers emptied trash cans and swept the short walkways of debris and dirt. He decided to go into the bank first, make his deposit, and then get something to eat. The steel and glass door were locked until the security guard saw him and pushed the button to let him in. "May I help you?" he asked as Leon approached the desk.

"Yes sir, my name is Leon Thompson, and I have a check, and I am new to the area, and I need to open an account," he said, nervously.

"Step right over there and see Miss Jones. She'll take care of you," the guard says to him.

"Thank you," Leon says as the guard leans his head left, and motions with his eyes towards the cashier sitting at her desk, away from the main counter. He gets to her desk, smiles back to her as she asks, "How may I help you?"

"Yes, my name is Leon Thompson, and I'm new in town, and I have a check, and I need to open an account."

"I can help you with that, welcome to Olee," she says to him. "Have a seat, and I'll need to see some ID, and the check."

"Yes ma'am," he says as he reaches into his cloth carry all and removes a 9"x12" envelope with all his important papers inside. He opens it, turns that end to the desk and several items slide out. Among them are his prison ID, social security card, expired Georgia driver's license, and the letter from his aunts with the check folded inside. He collects them, and one by one gives her the check, his social security card, and the expired driver's license. She carefully looks them over, and asks the obvious question, "What do you want to do with this check?"

"I want to make a deposit and establish an account. I don't have a place to stay yet, but I have some cash. This was my first stop," he answers.

"Good. These are certified funds, so that's no problem, but since you don't have an address, we'll probably need to establish a lock box. Did you want to open a savings and a checking account as well?" she asks earnestly.

"Sure, I'll need to pay for things, and I hope to find some work soon, so yes, all that," he says to her.

"Okay, I have some forms for you to sign, and we'll get you set up in the computer," she says to him. "What kind of work do you do?" she asks him next.

"All kinds of work," he says at first. "You know, general labor, warehouse. I don't have much training, or computer skills, so some entry level work. I just need to start somewhere," he offers.

"Be sure and check in at the temporary agency over on Beckwith Street. You can get some day work there. Plus, there are some places where you can rest your head near there for a small fee and pay by the day. It used to be rough over there, but they cleaned the area up good about a year ago. You should be okay," she said to him.

As she entered his personal information into the computer she noticed he was becoming fidgety, and nervous like, looking around, and seeming to want to ask her something of importance.

"Excuse me ma'am, is this going to take long? I probably need to go across the street to use the restroom," he says to her, obviously in distress.

"Oh, that won't be necessary." She waved to the guard who came over, and after a gesture towards a door near the back of the building by Miss Jones, he escorted Leon to the restroom, unlocking the door, yet looking at Leon with some sense of caution. Leon nodded as he passed Mr. Franklin and hurried into the stall. He did his business, washed his hands, looked into the mirror, blew a sigh of relief, and walked out. He returned to his seat, fighting back a comment, and answered a few more questions. She typed in the information, collected the signature cards, and went over the rules of banking with Olee National, and some state and federal guidelines. She turned the monitor towards him, and asked him to verify what she had entered, also explaining about the temporary address and the lock box, and the $25.00 fee. They would change the address as soon as he secured a suitable place to stay. She asked if he would need any more cash before she ran the deposit. He said that maybe a hundred or two would be enough to get him through a few days to pay for lodging, and a few things. She suggested two, and ran the deposit for $5,775.00, subtracting the lock box fee, and handed him the cash, and the temporary check and savings book. He took them, put the cash in his wallet, and the books in his envelope along with his other documents. She told him to be sure and ask for help as he moved around the city, and that Olee was a good place, and that people would make him feel welcome. She asked if he had any questions, and to feel free to come by the bank, or call if he had any problems with his account. He took her business card, stood with her, shook her hand, and walked over to Lulu's, thanking Mr. Franklin as he passed him before going out the door.

##

Lulu's café was established in 1971 by William Murphy and Edward Thomas, two hippies out of Atlanta with an acid dream, and an inheritance from Bill's grandfather. They wanted it to be a place for people who had smoked enough, dropped enough, or shot enough, to come, eat a decent meal, and perhaps engage in meaningful conversation. There would be farm fresh veggies and such, general liquid refreshments, and fresh breads from the local bakery. No alcohol was served, and drug use or possession was prohibited, though Ed was known to still take a toot or two of something occasionally. Bill was free of drugs after a five-year run. People would come from all over because it was safe and well run, and the 25-seat capacity made for just enough activity to hang with people you knew, or converse with a few new friends. The place did well for about seven years, and Bill and Ed decided, like so many of their early patrons, to move on to something else. Bill's first cousin, on his mother's side, who had been to college and earned a degree in business administration, bought the place from them. He established it as a mid-range eatery, basic southern breakfast and lunches served, and meat and potatoes with two vegetables for dinner, corn bread or rolls included. It had remained popular and didn't really have much competition from the fast-food places nearby. Lulu's was good, wholesome food, and atmosphere, served at a good price. Wednesday was family night, and kids under 12 ate for half off.

Leon had been out of prison close to five hours now, and he felt good. He was shocked when he saw the folded, $50 bill on the ground just before the door to Lulu's. He picked it up, looked around, and entered the café. It was almost 2pm, and about 12 people were left over from the lunch time rush. Aaron Beasley had added a few tables and chairs when he took over, and the dining area could now seat 46 comfortably, and was usually at that number for most of the lunch and dinner meals. He had done another remodel in 2011, opening the ceiling, enlarging the restrooms, and had a covered bench built near the entrance outside for four people to sit who were waiting for the next available table when there was a wait. Leon stepped up to the temporary, 'Seat Yourself' sign and went over to a two-seater near the back window. A waitress addressed him saying, "I'll be right back." He sat, placed his bag in the opposite seat, picked up the menu, and thought, "I'm free!" He took a deep breath, looked around, and made eye contact with a man in a coat and tie sitting across the room. The man nodded to him, and Leon nodded back. "Friendly," he thought. He became conscious that the fifty was still in his left hand, crinkled now, and he wasn't sure what to do with it. The slender waitress came back, and with a toothy grin says, "Hey, how ya doing? Welcome to Lulu's."

"Thank you, glad to be here."

"Would you like something to drink?" she asked him, looking him over like he was something good to eat.

"Ice water, I would love a glass of ice water," he says.

"Do you know what you want yet?" she asked as well.

"Not yet. I may do burger and fries, with a small house salad, though the fish sandwich looks good too. I'll know when you come back with the water," he says to her.

"That's fine. Take your time. Let me go take care of these other folks and I'll bring your water then," she offers, and walks off. It took her about six minutes to come back to him, after getting and placing the meals for two tables of four up near the front of the restaurant. She brought him his water, set it on the table, and looked directly at him with weary, darting eyes. "You ready?" she asked him.

"Think I'll go with the burger and fries, medium well, balsamic dressing on the salad, light. Easy on the condiments for the burger, but everything," he says. "No cheese."

She looks at him, writes the order, and asks if there's anything else, and winks at him.

"That will come later," he says. "Oh, by the way, I found this $50 bill on the ground just before I came in."

"An honest man," she says. "Geneva Henderson dropped it on her way out, she had just called and asked the manager if anyone had found it. She was frantic. You'll make an old woman happy today."

"Good. Do I give it to you, or the manager?" he asks her.

"No, hold on to it. I'll have him call her back and you can give it to her," she says to him.

"I don't want a big fuss."

"Well, people around here are decent. She'll want to meet you, fitting right in. Are you passing through, or new to the area?" she asks.

"New to the area. I've got to find a place," he answers.

"Wow, you're in luck. She has rental properties all over the place. I'm sure she'll hook you up," she says, dipping her head down, then up quickly, and winking again. "Honesty," she says.

"That's good to know, thank you."

"I'll go place your order. It shouldn't take long," she says.

"Good. I'm hungry, thanks."

##

Geneva arrived about the same time as the food. She spoke to several people when she came in, and the manager escorted her to where Leon sat. She gave him a big smile the closer she got to him, slowing her pace to allow the waitress to serve him his food. Leon stood to meet her, waiting that split second to see if she would offer her hand for him to grasp. She did.

"So, this is the young man," she said in greeting him. "My name is Geneva Henderson, and I want to thank you for your honesty."

"Yes ma'am, Leon Thompson. It didn't take much," he said as he hands her the bill.

"Thank you," she says. "May I pay for your lunch?"

"That will be fine, but not necessary. It was a simple act," he says to her.

"It would be my pleasure."

"In that case, I'll accept."

There was gentle laughter all around as the waitress steps up and says, "He needs a place to stay. He's new in town."

"Is that so?" Geneva responds, looking him over now.

"Yes ma'am. A small place. I'm looking for work too," he announces.

"Well, here's my card, call me after you eat, and maybe I can be of service," she offers graciously.

"That's kind of you. Thank you."

"Thank you again for your honesty."

They complete the handshake, she turns to walk off, and he sits to eat. The remaining crowd claps as if they've just witnessed a dramatic scene from a play.

Darla, the waitress, is all smiles as if she's directed the play, inwardly taking some credit for Leon's good fortune. She returns to one of her other tables, looking back to watch Leon bite into his burger, a bit of mustard and ketchup dripping just to the side of his lips. A couple of guests, upon leaving, walk by Leon's table and give him a nod, and a smile to let him know they appreciate his good deed. He acknowledges their greeting, but continues to eat, string- pouring ketchup on his fries. He loosens up a bit more in his chair, feeling better about his choice to come here, to Olee, and believing it all would work out nicely.

##

Leon paused after a few bites of the burger. This felt good. He grabbed a few fries, being careful not to get ketchup on his fingers, and put them into his mouth. He chewed and picked up the knife and fork to stir the salad. He then punched at it with the fork, securing enough green, orange, and red for a mouthful, and chewed on that. Darla came to check if he was okay and went on her way through the kitchen door to Leon's left. He wondered if anyone could tell he was just released from prison, a man with a past that didn't look good on paper, but whose actions, generally, were acceptable. He'd gotten into trouble, and spent time in jail before, but most didn't view him as a bad boy until he hurt Karen and caused the death of their unborn child. It would have been one thing if he had only hit her, but he beat her, and the testimony in court by her, and the restraint necessary to keep her father, Raymond, from killing Leon was outsized. He was put into protective custody, and Raymond had to go visit family in Toledo, Ohio until the trial was over. Fortunately, Karen was healthy and strong, twenty-four years old, and recovered from the incident, but the rest of the family, and the community, for that matter, never looked at Leon as someone they could trust after that. Obviously, he had snapped in some way and was forever changed for the worse, they thought. Of course, he had thought about it, and processed it with peers in prison, but there was no alcohol or drug abuse, or mental illness in his background, so something else had happened to him. He was sure the next few years of his life would give him answers, or so he hoped.

##

As he finished up his meal and sat for a moment Leon felt happy inside. So far so good. He looked around for a pay phone, or any other public one, as he saw some patrons use their personal phones. He knew he would have to ask someone if there was a phone store nearby so he could rent one to call Ms. Henderson and tend to other issues as they came up in making his rounds.

"Finished darling?" Darla asked when she got to his table.

"Yes, thank you. That was great."

"Do you want a piece of pie, coffee, or anything else?" she continues.

"No thank you, I'm good. I don't know how to ask this, but did she leave you a tip?"

"She did. You're fine darling."

"Okay, good. I do have one thing if you can point me in the right direction? I need a cell phone."

"Sure darling, Que Phone, next to the barber shop. Go out the front door, take a left, go about two blocks to Moore street, and you'll see the church on the corner. Walk past the church parking lot and take a right at Sims. You'll start to see the business district and all the shops. You'll see the pizza place over on the left side of the street about thirty yards away, and around the corner, to your left is Byrd's Barber shop and Que Phone is right next to it," she tells him.

"That's great. Thank you for taking care of me. Great food, great place. I'm sure I'll be back," he says to her.

"Okay, do that. We'll see you next time. Good luck."

"Thanks."

Leon gets up, grabs his bag, and starts the next phase of his journey.

##

Walking free like this was pleasurable. This was not like the track because even though you were outdoors, you were confined by designated lines, and your level of access. He followed the path outlined by Darla and arrived at Que Phone in ten minutes. He waved at a couple of guys in the barber shop and noted that he would probably need a cut next week. He pushed on the door, which was locked, so the clerk at the counter buzzed him in.

"General precaution," she said. "How are you today?"

"Fine, fine. I need a phone. My ID is outdated, but I do have my social security card. I don't have a residence yet, but I do have money on me and in the bank. I need to see about a place to stay, and I have someone I'm supposed to call," he gives her all at once.

"Fine, that's good. I can hook you up, no problem. Did you just get out?" she asked, not being intrusive, but more as an icebreaker.

"Well, actually I did. Ten years. I'm trying to get situated here if it works out," he opens up to her.

"You should be okay. This is a good place. I've been here about nine month, and I like it so far."

Leon's eyes go to the wall behind Shinicqua, and to her left, where he can step up and get a closer look at the offerings.

"What kind of phone did you have before?" she asks him.

"I can't remember. It was pretty basic: calls, texts, I don't think it had a camera," he tries to recall.

"Aw man, they do everything now, and you can get a good one for a little over a hundred a month.

Internet, movies, you name it," she says.

"Okay, what do I need to do?" he asks her.

"Let me see the ID you have, and I can go over a few plans and phones."

He hands her the expired driver's license first. She takes it and says, "Oh, that's right around the corner. If you don't have any outstanding tickets or warrants, you should be able to get them renewed. Do you want to do that first and come back?" she asks him.

"Well, let's see. I need to make that call..."

"Okay, why don't you do this, I have a phone here you can use. Maybe that's your first move, then we can see what's next?"

"That sounds good. Okay."

She hands him the phone, shows him how to make a call, and points over to an area where he can sit and talk. She gives him a pen and a piece of paper for notes. He takes a seat, looks a little puzzled, but makes the call.

"Hi, Ms. Henderson, this is Leon Thompson, we met at the restaurant today, and you told me to give you a call if I needed some help."

"Yes, my $50 man, what do you need?" she asks.

"I need a place to stay, and some work."

"Today?"

"Yes, well, a place to stay. Work maybe tomorrow."

"Where are you?"

"Que Phone. But I need to get my driver's license renewed as well."

"Do you know where the DDS is located?"

"Yes, the nice lady here told me it's nearby."

"What kind of work can you do?"

"Probably general labor right now. I have a few skills, but I need to start off slow."

"Okay, I'm going to send my niece down to pick you up in about an hour. Check on the license thing, but don't get a phone yet."

"Yes ma'am."

"Okay, I'll see you later."

"Okay."

Leon's head is spinning now. Things are happening, and like he's heard, this is a good place, with good people.

He hands her the phone, pen, and paper scrap, and thanks her.

"Yes, I need to see about the license thing first," he tells her.

"That's good. Okay," she says as she points up the street to the Walker Building. "Have a good day. Come back when you're ready."

"I will," he says to her, and walks out the door.

#

The Department of Driver Services shares space with the county tax commissioner's office. It's a good space with three service windows, and adequate space for employees to walk back and forth, behind and between them to access the copy and fax machines. Usually, only two windows are in use most days, except at the first of the year, most of March, and the first week of every month. There are chairs for up to ten people, and a work bench by the window to prepare forms, and check paperwork, or make calls. Leon walks up to the information desk, and the security guard greets him.

"May I hep you?" he says, a bit affected.

"Yes sir, my name is Leon Thompson, and I need to get my driver's license renewed."

"Okay, step over there and get a number and have a seat. They'll be with you shortly. Have some ID ready to show them."

"Yes sir, thank you."

Leon pulls the number 28 and sees only two other people waiting. The overhead digital counter shows 26. Leon takes a seat and hears the number 27 called out. An older gentleman steps up, and after an exchange of papers, and questions and answers, and the clerk taking some cash from him, he walks from the desk smiling, waving his renewed license. The process took about eight minutes.

"28."

Leon hears his number and sees the change overhead. He steps up to the counter and smiles at the gentleman clerk.

"May I help you?" he asks.

"Yes, my name is Leon Thompson, and I need to renew my driver's license."

"Do you have the old one, and your social security card, and a bill to show residence?"

"Here, I have the old one, and my social, but I'm new in town and don't have a place yet."

"2000! Wow, where have you been?" the clerk exclaims.

"Away. I let a few things slip back then."

The clerk runs his social, looks at Leon, and back to the monitor.

"Man, okay, okay. Let's see," the clerk begins. "Good news and bad news. The good news is you can renew them, but the bad news is it's going to cost you, and you have to take both tests over, written and driving."

"How much?"

"Let's see. $220.00 renewal, ticket from 2001, $357.00, and the new license is $40.00. So, $617.00."

"When can I do it?"

"Not today. You need to establish residence, pay the fees, pass the written test, and have someone bring you for the driving portion. If you get a place today, you could come back Wednesday for the written. Here's the booklet to study, or you can go online. When you pass that, you can take the driving on Friday, or Saturday. We're closed on Thursday. This will give you time to get your stuff together."

"Awh man, this is great. Do I bring cash, money order?"

"Either is fine, debit card."

"Oh, I need one of those. Good, I need to go back to the bank tomorrow anyway."

"Okay, you're all set. We open at 8:30 and close at 4:00."

"Okay. Thanks."

Leon is all happy, giddy even. Another success, and another helpful person. When he walks outside he realizes that Ms. Henderson didn't describe her niece. About 30 minutes had passed since they talked so he thought he would just go sit in the park and wait. She would probably be looking here first, or back over by the phone store. It was all right together so she would be able to spot him. He was thirsty and went into the store on the corner to buy a bottle of water. He returned to the park and took a seat near a statue of a Mr. Thomas Walker, former major and civic leader, the plaque said. He drank about half of the bottle of water, laughed aloud, and stretched wide eagle on the bench, knocking his bag to the ground. 'Thank you, Jesus,' he shouted to himself, head down so as not to draw attention to himself. After about ten minutes a white car pulls in near the entrance to the park, and the lady driver, about his age, or maybe older, looks out her window at the three other persons there, a young couple, and a lady probably on a late work break. Madalyn then looks directly at him and says, "Mr. Thompson." He waves a yes, gets his bag, and heads for the car, smiling.

##

Madalyn Davis was a retired army veteran, widowed with two kids, ages 10 and 12. She served one tour each in Iraq and Afghanistan. Her husband, Kirk, was killed subduing a crazed gunman on a train from Washington, DC back in 2011. He was a retired service person as well, and his training prevented an international incident as several students from North Korea were the intended targets. Madalyn, at 46, was a fit and competent manager of the rental properties Ms. Henderson had acquired over the past 37 years. She was known to be fair and compassionate, but a businessperson never-the-less. She adhered to agreements and expected the renters to comply as well.

On approach, Leon was struck by her short hair and attractive good looks. She was a beauty, and he had a reaction that he didn't expect to occur so soon.

"Mr. Thompson, get in, I'm Madalyn."

Leon froze for a moment and said a prayer of forgiveness. He moved to the passenger side of the utility vehicle and opened the door.

He noticed the war wound, and surgical scar on the inside of her leg, thigh down, past her left knee, and slid into his seat.

"How ya doing?" she asked, her bubbly personality coming forth.

"You know, I'm good. Thanks for coming to pick me up. How did you know it was me?" he asks her.

"Easy. You were the only other male, and you looked up as the car came near the park. You were looking for something, he already had it."

"Wow, that's pretty good," he observes.

"Training."

"How so?" he asks.

"Military. 22 years. Stealth duty, survey the area," she offers.

"That's great."

They both go silent, as she signals, and turns up Walker Road heading to Westmont, 6 miles away.

"I notice a lot of Walker around here," Leon says.

"Sure, Thomas Walker, great man. Helped a lot of people. Died in a fire trying to save his mother. The fire chief told him not to go into the house, but he was known to do things others couldn't do. It was his mother; he adored that woman."

"Great, but tragic?" he comments.

"Oh, there are plenty more examples, and you'll hear one occasionally, from the old timers around here. He was a good man. A man of service. So, tell me about Leon?" she asks.

"Not much to tell. Born and raised in Hardison, up near Atlanta. My father and grandfather were good men, good workers. My mother was a teacher. One older sister. I got into some trouble a few times, then really messed up and I've been gone away for the past ten years."

"What kind of trouble?" she asks him.

"As a teenager, just stupid stuff, property violations, and some stealing. A few fights with some older people. Nothing too bad, but then I hit my girlfriend, and she lost the baby."

"Bad boy, or bad breaks?"

"You know, I don't know. Sometimes things just went wrong. I didn't intend for them to happen, but choices I guess. I became the wrong crowd when I had so much good given to me," he owns.

"What kind of good?" she asks.

"Values mostly. Good living examples by my parents, and the old folks in the neighborhood. Such good, decent people who lived well together."

"So, we can trust you?"

"Probably. I feel that I can now have the kind of life I always wanted. I'm in no hurry, I'm just trying to do God's will."

"That's probably a good thing," she says. "So, what will you need?"

"Just a small room with facilities. I need to find work and see where I am in a few months. Eventually I need to think in terms of a career, I guess. But for now, just to be able to show up and do a job is plenty. I'm sure my skills and talents will take me somewhere as time goes on."

"Great. We have a room, and a job for you."

"That's great. Where and what?" he asks her.

"Mrs. Henderson will go over all that with you, and her husband, William, will show you around. They will be good, basic accommodations, and that will get you started."

"Sounds like a plan. I'm ready."

##

Prison had taught Leon three things, when to lie, how to survive in close quarters with men of varying interests, and what skill to use, and when. He started out in a high security penitentiary, and after six years, with just a few infractions, was moved to medium for two years, one at low, and finally at discharge was in the camp area. He read a lot, had various jobs, and generally stayed away from the criminals, as it were. He didn't intend on that becoming his life's work, so he followed the rules, took care of himself, and was preparing for release almost from the beginning. At thirty-five he was healthy enough, and smart enough to be able to put together a good life, despite the bad aspects of his past. Once he got a break, he kept thinking, he was not going to let it slip away. He wasn't sure about any family type goals, but he did want to have a companion, and if marriage was a possibility, he was willing to give it a try. He and Karen had been good for two years, and other relationships had been okay, so he did have practice at being a mate. He would need some guidance, and especially if the woman had kids around. In prison, early on, he did have some therapy about his situation, but no useful answers came of it. One summary simply said, "Bad actor. He'll probably violate again. Lacks impulse control." Though rudimentary and assessed on a young man of twenty-five under stress, with limited outside interests, Leon had accepted the report and left it at that. He couldn't make any promises as to future behavior anyway. After all, they were the experts.

Madalyn sized him up at 5'10" 175lbs. shoe size 10, and in good health. He had a good, square face, and gentle eyes, and seemed to have a good IQ based on their conversation on the way to Westmont, the Henderson's estate. Geneva had thought he was okay when she met him but bared watching simply because he was new to the area. They would have him do some basic clean-up work, and help with the general maintenance of the houses, and two apartment buildings. Plus, he could help William re-organize the warehouse. It wouldn't take long to get a good assessment of his true character.

"Here we are," Madalyn announced as they turned onto 446 Westmont Circle. It was a sprawling property of 18 acres, with a huge main house, guest quarters, and the storage facility. Leon took note of the four vehicles parked to the side of the house, lining a drive that led to a garage underneath the house. He wasn't sure how he would fit into all this, but he was grateful for how things were playing out so far.

We sat there resting, knowing who and what we were,
no chance to imagine what was not,
me, and the four empty chairs.

William, who was outside near one of the cars, was having an animated conversation with a man just as large as he was, surely 6'4", near 300lbs. He was holding some papers, and the other man would point to them occasionally, stepping away, then turning to face William again. This time the man shrugged his shoulders, smiled, and they shook hands. The man walked around him, got into the front car, and drove off. William took out his cell phone, pushed contact, and Geneva answered.

"That clown," William began. "He's in, but I could only get a promise of $60,000.00. That will leave us about twenty thousand short. How do you want to handle it?"

"Let me think about it. Madalyn's pulling into the driveway with the guy," she observes.

"Oh, I did not hear them," William says.

"Are you coming in?" she asks him.

"Give me a minute. I have two calls to make."

"Okay," she says.

##

Geneva came out to greet them, giving Madalyn a big hug and shaking Leon's hand again.

"Mr. Thompson, good to see you again."

"Ms. Henderson, likewise."

"It's Mrs. Henderson," she corrected him. "You'll meet my husband William shortly."

"Good. Lucky man."

"Okay, you all come on in, and let's talk," Geneva responds.

She addressed them as if they were a couple, which Leon thought was noteworthy. Leon slung his bag over his right shoulder and followed the ladies into the house. Upon entering Madalyn excused herself and went upstairs. Geneva showed Leon to the living room, which was ornate and crystalline with padded chairs and old master type paintings of families in various action settings. She offered Leon a chair, and asked if he needed something to drink, or a snack. He declined and made himself comfortable thinking, "this is new!" Madalyn returned, sat in a chair next to Leon, and now William enters from a basement door, his large frame immediately overtaking the room.

"Hey everybody, who have we here?" he bellows.

Leon stands and introduces himself.

"I heard you did a good deed today and we would like to do you one in turn," William says as he takes a seat next to Geneva on a large, cushy sofa.

Leon sits and enters the conversation.

"Well, as I was telling Madalyn I was just released from prison this morning. I was in for ten years. I was charged with assault, and involuntary manslaughter as I had beat up my girlfriend, Karen, who was four months pregnant. She lost the baby. I had been in some trouble before and have been in prison for a total of eleven years. I held various jobs, stayed out of trouble, and chose Olee because it seemed small enough, yet progressive enough for me to start over. I have some money in the bank, and I'm looking for work and a place to stay."

"Good," William responds. "We need help with our business operations, grunt work, as it were, but work, nevertheless. Maddie runs everything, and I fix what needs fixing. That would become your job."

"I can give you my best," Leon says. "I start off slow and work up to my skill and talent level. That's what I have to offer."

"That's good; let's give it a try. If it works, it works. If not, well...Hey, It's almost dinner time. Why don't you eat with us, and I'll take you to your apartment afterwards," William says to Leon.

"Sounds great," Leon responds.

##

Geneva had prepared a basic meal of salmon, rice, and broccoli. Corn bread was available if anyone was so inclined. They sat in the dining area, had modest conversation about general events, finished eating, and put away the dishes, to be washed later. Geneva wished Leon good luck, and Madalyn said she would probably see him tomorrow. Leon and William head for the door, out to the pick-up truck, and ride off.

"What all do you need to get set up?" William asked him.

"I need to go to the DDS tomorrow, get a cell phone, and whatever food, furnishings and general living products for the apartment," Leon answered.

"The apartment's furnished, but you will need to get your personal items. We start work at 7:30. I'll pick you up and show you around to our properties, then we can get your license stuff worked out. Madalyn will give you a company phone, but of course you can get a private one if you need to. You'll be on call in the evenings because I usually leave the shop about four. It's quiet around here, and we screen our guests thoroughly, you included. Not much we don't know about you already. Okay, do you have any questions so far?"

"You know, I'm easy. As time goes on I'll have them, of course, but right now I'm good."

"Okay."

#

151 Tyler Street was Leon's new address, and he proudly showed the clerk at the DDS office, as well as the teller who waited on him at the bank his agreement papers for a one-year lease. William had gotten him settled into his apartment, and they worked a few hours this morning. They were to meet Madalyn at the larger of the two apartment buildings over on Jefferson Street at 2 o'clock, and she would give Leon a phone at that time and show him his duties there. William had another appointment, so Maddie agreed to drop Leon off at his place after work.

"What do you think of everything so far?" Maddie asked him when they locked the shop door and headed for her car.

"It's pretty overwhelming. This is what I would dream about in prison. You all have been so nice. I just want to earn my way," he says to her.

"A day at a time, as they say," she responded. "Tomorrow, I want you to do the maintenance checks at your complex the way William showed you, and I'll pick you up at 10 to go for a house inspection."

"Okay, I'll be ready."

"Have a good night," she said when he got out of the car and walked to his apartment door, to open it for the first time himself.

He removed the key chain from his pocket and froze right there on the landing. He looked around at the four acres, landscaped property, and the 16 units, then said a prayer of thanks to himself. He knew this was real, and that everything would be okay. He stepped in, awkwardly, went to his knees after closing the front door, and said 'thank you.' He got up, sat in a chair, closed his eyes, and went to sleep for about an hour. When he awoke, he took the time to look over the place, which had been remodeled a year ago. It looked larger and brighter than what he could tell last night, and he was pleased with the way the one bedroom, one bath unit was apportioned. Looking around further, all he could see that was needed were some work clothes, and his favorite hygiene products. Otherwise, he was set.

The knock on the door was somewhat unnerving as he had no reason to expect a visitor, and no one, he thought, knew he was William's assistant, and worked for Henderson Properties, the owners of the residence here. He looked through the peep hole and saw that it was Maddie.

"Have you had dinner yet?" she asked when he opened the door.

"No, I haven't. What do you have there?" he asked her.

"Best noodles and spring rolls in town!"

"I'm in! Come on in," he says as he waves his open hand to welcome her to his domain, which actually was part hers as one third partner in the business.

##

Karen had since moved on and married a military man. They have a six-year-old son, and live near the Army base in Columbus, Georgia. Karen teaches first graders at the post elementary school, and Gerald, her husband, was recently promoted to Major, after returning from duty in Ramstadt, Germany. He is a small arms expert who had developed sight enhancers for use in the desert. They were happy together and both enjoyed their career paths.

Karen rarely thought of Leon, and what happened. She had only wished that she had not called him a 'punk, hoe, or 'B' word, after seeing him with Sarah Tomlinson, her best friend, at the mall the Saturday before it happened. They looked so happy, and playful together, and her jealousy overtook her. She became angry when Sarah laughed it off as no big deal, and that Karen needed to know that her 'man' had a lot of 'girlfriends' and other babies, and that she was nothing special to him. When Karen told her father, Raymond, about seeing Leon with Sarah he advised her to stop going with him. Karen had tried to talk to Leon about their relationship, and asked if he intended on marrying her, and be faithful, but he said he was too young to settle down, and he needed to have a lot of 'friends.' Plus, he already had seven kids, and she would have to get used to that. That's when she called him out and inflamed his anger. She did not expect him to hit her, nor did she feel responsible for his bad behavior. She was glad, at the time, that he went to jail, and that she did not have his baby.

##

Leon enjoyed dinner with Maddie, and their conversation about the people who lived in this complex. Most were working people who didn't stand out, average age around forty-five, who went about their business with little fanfare. There was another contingent, retired, or semi-retired, who were quiet and unassuming as well based on a reduced need for external stimuli. The courtyard afforded a place for them to sit and talk at various times of the day, and because the grounds were so well maintained there was always a sense of serenity and calm to the area. Some read, there was an artist who painted at times, but generally it was a place for peace and stillness.

Along with the renter's packet Maddie gave him an employment agreement, pay and general duties information, and state and federal workplace guidelines. They all were standard, and acceptable, with Maddie explaining to him that William would have some other items to discuss with him. The evening had gone well, and Maddie left about 7:30.

The next morning Leon woke about six, cleaned up, and put on his one change of clothes. William picked him up at seven and they were busy all day with work, getting a truck ready for Leon's use, shopping for food and clothes, and completed a repair at Madalyn's house. The rest of the week was full and busy, and Leon passed his tests, got his license, and drove around town most of Sunday by himself. William and Maddie had compared notes and agreed he had done well with the assignments he had been given, but would need at least another week, maybe two, of William's direct supervision to get used to the routine, and to face more challenges. Also, he needed to be introduced to various vendors, so they could get to know him. Leon was feeling happy and grateful for the experience thus far, and just wanted to prove himself worthy of all the good that had come his way.

##

Madalyn and her two kids, Don, and Catherine, returned from vacation the third week of August, allowing for three days to prepare for the new school year. Geneva and William would not return for another month, extending their stay on Hilton Head Island in South Carolina. The reports from Leon, and about his work from others, were favorable as he had completed the preparations on the Oak Street houses that had been put up for sale. 247 was under contract, and 253 was being shown by agents daily. The former renters had moved out in July, and it was a matter of time before it was under contract as well. Leon had taken great pride in completing the punch list items, and his skills and attention to detail were evident, though he did have to call in an electrician to refit an outlet box after his failed attempt to connect some wiring properly at 247.

People around town were getting used to his friendly smile and helpfulness. He didn't go out of his way to be helpful, but if something were obvious to him, he would step up. Sometimes he could perceive a need, or spot something others had missed. That's what Russell Herman had told William about Leon, and this special sense he seemed to have. Appropriately, Geneva and William, as well as Maddie, were glad that after only four months of employment Leon was doing a great job in their absence.

#

Maddie returned to work on Tuesday, having registered the kids back in school on Monday. They generally walked the mile and a half to school, and most days Maddie would pick them up after. They were good kids and were developing nicely during this phase of their lives.

#

Outwardly, Maddie didn't show the scars from Kirk's death, but they were there. They had been friends since high school and married at

21. The kids came late, after they had established their military careers, and everyone took note of how they cared for each other. They never served on the same post, or in the same theater, but that didn't put any more stress on the relationship. They were united, and that was that. She had teared up once, in talking to Leon because he had those same gentle eyes, and easy manner of living like Kirk, and, oddly, seemed to understand the challenges of being a single, working parent. Although she had a lot of flexibility in her schedule, and ability to move around, it was still a tough job. She had not dated since Kirk's passing, and Leon wasn't sure where a woman fit into his future plans.

OLIVER HENDERSON

He had stopped praying. He was afraid but knew this day would come. He was sixty-five years old and had maxed his sentence. They couldn't give him more time. He had to go. He said goodbyes to old cons like himself and didn't look back after the C.O. gave him his satchel. There was nothing left here for him to do. He would have to move on. He would have to live "out there."

It had been thirty-one years since the time stood still. He was guilty and convicted and he had a number. He would become an inmate, not to be trusted, not to be valued, just someone who used to be, or could have been. He would need watching.

It was the third of January 1986, cold, moist air dripping through the fog. He needed one more hit, another fix, then he could go home for a spell, rest, answer a few questions from his mother, then nod off. That's what he hoped to do until Gena called his name. He tried to avoid her, she was trouble, but he needed another hit.

"Yo, what's up?" she had cried out to him. "Give me something!"

He tried to walk away, but she was on him like the plague of 1667. It was going to be messed up either way, so he turned to her and smiled.

"Baby girl, what's up?" he shot back to her.

"Come on, let's go over here and get this money. It's a sweet lick. Your boy has got ten thousand on him; I've been with him all day."

"Come on Gena don't do that. I've got to get well."

"I'm telling you he's drunk. It's free money." She opens her handbag and shows him a lot of bills, fifties, and twenties. "I'm telling you it's money man, sweet."

"I can't do that, just give me fifty and I'll straighten it later," he says to her.

"It's money man, he's up there drunk. You better get you some," she says to him.

"Which room?" Oliver asks.

"15," she says to him.

*

No, but it is cold, and the earth is frozen, and the place where it was, had to be the squirrel, for one day I caught him there, hiding a piece of bread, there, where I threw it.

*

When the police found him, two days later, Oliver was in a joint over on Lucky Street. He was in a chair, nodding, next to the fifth pool table, the one he played all the time. A couple of other hustlers were there, but it was calm. No one moved when the officers drew their weapons on approach. They'd already heard the story of what happened.

"Oliver Henderson," the tall black one spoke, reaching down to push Oliver's left shoulder to wake him. He stirred but stayed into his nod.

"Oliver, we need to talk to you," he said again, this time more forceful with the push.

Oliver kind of opened his eyes but drooped back into his nod. The second officer, Larry Owens, moved closer as well, reached down to pull Oliver up from the chair, and this time Oliver woke and stayed woke. He looked around, shook it off, and sat back down. He then asked, "What's up fellows?"

"Well, you're going to tell us. We need you to stand back up and keep your hands where we can see them. You're under arrest for the murder of Larry Jenkins."

He thought it a dream, that he was finally getting busted for some other crimes he'd committed, but he was no murderer. He was a thief; he just took stuff to get stuff. Generally, he liked people.

**

No family or friends were waiting on him, there had been no calls or letters for a long time. He would start this journey alone carrying his satchel, and the money that was in the bank. He had decided on Greensboro, a small-town west of Atlanta. He had studied the area and felt comfortable about its political make up. He could blend in with the other seniors, retired with modest means. He had secured a one-bedroom unit in a newly opened five-story complex on Beckwith Street, Harlan Village. It was part of a chain of hotels that was moving into the booming senior residential sector popular in this part of the state. This development offered four and six hundred square feet apartments designed with enough room for a single person or a couple who loved each other. The construction was bright and modern, with security features for an older population. There was a courtyard and pool, and enough common use amenities that facilitated interaction, yet respected boundaries, and enough staff to accommodate certain needs. Meals were prepared, though one could always have a snack in their own unit. It was a perfect setup for Oliver to start his new life. It would take time for him to adjust, but this was an ideal setting.

The hired car had taken Oliver to get clothes, hygiene products and a few other personal items. The driver was a good man, and hearing Oliver out about his situation took the time to allow him to look at things and soak up the area. Oliver paid him accordingly and they arrived at one o'clock. Mr. Thornton met them in the driveway and welcomed Oliver to his new home.

"Mr. Henderson, glad to finally meet you. Welcome to Harlan Village. Let me help you with your bags."

"Yes, thank you."

Thornton put the four bags on a cart rack and waved to the driver. The driver then gave Oliver a thumbs up and drove off.

"Okay, come this way. Did you have a good trip?"

"It's been good," Oliver responded.

"So, everything is in order, let's get you up to the third floor, 307 is your unit, corner as requested with a full view of the woods and lake. Were you able to get lunch?"

"Yes."

Thornton and Oliver were about the same height, both stood tall and certain. Mr. Thornton, however, was feeling anxious about the new resident's short answers and wondered if he had something to hide. All his personal information checked out well and there was no reason to suspect anything untoward, yet this was a kind of peace and reserve that was new for Thornton as he generally managed properties where there was a lot of commotion. He too was adjusting to a new setting. When they got to the unit and Thornton opened the door Oliver paused before going in, looking directly at Thornton, and announcing, "You know I did thirty-one years in federal prison."

"Yes, I know who you are. It shouldn't be a problem. You're the fourth resident to move here, you have status."

"Thank you," Oliver responded.

**

As Oliver unpacked and stored the few items he had with him it was the collection of fifteen miniature glass figurines that gave him the most joy and comfort. They had survived the last ten years of incarceration when he was transferred to a low security level. He had been in the system so long he had acquired certain personal items that even though they could be construed as borderline weapons he was able to keep them. He did not display them, nor did he talk about them much. The guards knew they kept him calm.

*

"What are these?" he had asked the young heroin dealer years ago.

"Nature's creatures," he had said.

"I can see that," Oliver responded, "but why do you have them?"

"They keep me sane in this insane world. After I'm out hustling all day and night when I get to my apartment, I put them on the desk and look at them."

"Why?"

"I must take care of them. I don't want them to get hurt."

"You mean broken or cracked?"

"No, hurt. They represent the way I feel inside. Out there I must lie, cheat, carry pistols, and fight with folks to make my money. When I survive and get home I take care of them."

"You mean you take care of your soul?"

"Yes. Strong, fragile, beautiful."

"Why do you want to give them to me?" Oliver asked the young man.

"Because I knew Gena, and I know you took her fall. She was my mother, and she wanted you to have these. My father told me to find you when I got knocked out and give them to you. She died fifteen years ago of AIDS."

"Shouldn't you keep them?"

"No. She wrote a letter. It told what happened that night, and she prayed for you all the time because you kept your word. She got clean after that night and stayed straight until she died."

"Why did you get into the drug business?"

"I don't know, but when I get out I'm not going back to it, and I make that promise to you. So, keep the figurines and pray that I keep my promise the way you have."

"I will."

AUDREY PETERSON

"He went there often, and she would wait for him. He had forgotten how it started but it was in full force. He at times wanted to stop, but he could not. Her allure was powerful, and he had to give in. She was expensive but worth it. He knew it would end badly but he needed her now more than ever. She was the green-eyed lady with no home."

Fifteen years is a long time to be in prison. It's a long time to be anywhere doing something you dislike, but she had earned the right to be there. Her crime was costly, and payback would take time. She had time starting August 25th, 2013, a hot day in South Georgia, with a hundred dollars in her small purse. She was thirty-six years old and didn't have a friend. It would stay that way for a while here in Thomaston. People remembered what she did to Floyd years ago, he was a good man. He should not have died that way, but he should have known better. She already had a 'reputation.'

Audrey Peterson was a whore and a drunk, you couldn't say it any better. She was bad news until you read the funny papers if you know what I mean. She would trap you and take you down roads only for the mean, or hard hearted. She didn't know any better, it started early with her father, she was not supposed to be daddy's girl. He knew better. It's still a mystery how he died. Audrey never talked about it, not even with the county shrinks. She said she had no feelings about it, and she didn't remember her mother. She would make her way in life and be okay. She had learned about the world at the age of seven; she knew how things worked. It would be okay she would say to anyone who would listen to her story; few did. It was too painful.

*

Eric's career at the bank had been modest up to this point. As lead of the mortgage department he earned a good salary, had dated some good women, but had not married. He wanted a family, but the right one had not come along. He was devoted to the bank and the community, volunteered where he could help out, enjoyed his friends, and played golf most weekends. He was studious and upright, never misspent a dime, and had sound spiritual beliefs, as it were. He did not attend church, which some had tried to get him to do, so people accepted him for who he was, just a good decent guy. Laura Turner, however, would invite him to Bible study on Wednesday nights because he was so well read and insightful in discussions about different topics. She enjoyed his company and still hoped he would pick her if he ever decided to settle down. She liked his big, strong presence at six-one, two hundred-fifteen pounds. They could take care of each other, she thought, and she would love to have a couple of babies by him; a boy and a girl would be perfect.

*

Audrey went straight to the bank from the bus depot. She didn't stand around or reminisce about being back home, she would do things differently now. She was older and wiser and had a new life. She wanted to deposit the insurance check, make some investments, and get to Aunt Minnie's house. That's where she would be living.

Eric stood at the front door of the bank greeting customers. When Audrey appeared he gave her the standard 'Good Morning Ma'am' and gestured for her to come on in. He didn't recognize her at first but as she walked by him he had a tingle of physical reaction. He watched her walk over to the customer service desk and almost allowed the door to close on the older couple about to come in. He smiled and apologized to Mr. and Mrs. Greeson. They smiled back and walked on in.

Susan Hardaway greeted Audrey Peterson and asked her to have a seat. She asked why she was there, and Audrey showed her an envelope and pulled the check and some other personal documents out to show her. Susan looked them over with a focused attention, smiled warmly, and mentioned Mr. Gaines as the vice president who would come over to meet her shortly. Susan pulled out some forms from the desk drawer, enlivened her computer screen with the mouse, and began to more officially welcome Audrey back to Thomaston after getting more personal history from her. Audrey felt more relaxed, yet uncomfortable about this new chapter of her life. She could also feel the eyes of Mr. Gaines lustfully looking upon her. After speaking to another customer who had completed their banking business for the day Eric walked over and spoke to Susan and the lady sitting at her desk.

"Yes, Mr. Gaines, this is Ms. Audrey Peterson. She's here to open several accounts. She was born and raised here and is coming back after being away awhile," Susan reports.

"Mrs. Peterson, good to meet you. Thanks for choosing Southern for your banking needs," he says rather officiously.

"Thank you, but I'm not married," Audrey corrects.

"Sorry," he says. "Susan will take good care of you, and if there's anything I can do let her know; I manage the mortgage department if you're looking to buy a house," he says, trying to remain professional but entertaining more personal thoughts.

After about an hour Audrey had secured a checking and savings account, two fifty-thousand-dollar certificates of deposit, and a sense of belonging as Susan made her feel at home with her efficient yet personal demeanor. Susan had also helped Audrey find a car service to take her out to Aunt Minnie's house.

CHAPTER TWO

It was a hot and sticky morning, and Audrey could feel the sweat collected by the white cotton blouse she wore as she stood in front of the bank. There was a soft breeze that brought attention to the faded jeans she had on, not too tight, but clingy, nevertheless. She had slept in a nice Vacation Express hotel last night, showered, and put on the fresh clothes she wore today. She had left a fifty-dollar deposit and had enough cash from her banking to satisfy a few days stay if necessary. She wasn't sure what she would find at Aunt Minnie's, but her cousin Robert had sent a message, before she left prison, of where to find the house key and general operations information as to alarm codes, maintenance contacts, etc., and that he would come to meet her when she arrived. The car service arrived in five minutes, and she was taken to 155 Beckwith Street to a neat fifties style ranch ten minutes from the center of town.

*

One fifty-five Beckwith Street faced the sunset at thirty-five degrees southwest. It was a three-sided brick that had been remodeled twice for space and appearance over the past forty years. Horace and Minnie didn't have kids but enjoyed a full, vigorous life with parties and get togethers for family, friends, and business associates. When the car pulled in front of the house Audrey could recall birthdays and holidays spent here, and the joy that was present within its walls. Horace was a big, jovial man and Minnie was a crackerjack who loved to tell a good, clean joke and would start laughing just before the punch line. She would usually have a drink in her hand, but she never seemed drunk or out of sorts.

Audrey asked the driver if she could sit for a moment, not long, but just enough time to soak in her journey of the last couple of years. She was no longer a convict, she could come and go as she pleased, she was healthy, and the resentments, hurt, and shame of life on the streets for two years was like a dream that disturbed you, but upon awakening it was mist upon the lake, easily drifting upwards in a disappearing moment of clarity. You were in a safe place now, there was enough distance that your truth was palatable, and you could face up to anyone and state, "Yes, I have lived, but I should have died!"

She gave the driver an extra twenty and walked to the side of the house and found the baggie in the bushes that held a set of keys and a note. It was moist from an earlier rain, but the contents were protected from exposure. A tear of gratitude rolled down the left side of her face that led to an all-out guttural cry as she appreciated how lucky she was that she really had a chance for a new life of trust and direction. She was glad the last five years of incarceration had gone by so fast and that she believed and acted as if good things could really happen for her. She was a different person, and worth having a good life. It was no longer a theory; she could live it!

*

Eric continued to be intrigued by the new customer as he completed his workday. There was an air of familiarity, but he couldn't quite place it until he read in her file that she listed 155 Beckwith as her address, which he knew was the Hawkins house. Slowly it came to him that Minnie's niece had gone off to prison years ago, but moreover he recalled a wild night of his where a young woman about town had rejected his advances and how angry he had become. Then at a party weeks later she was there, more friendly, and they had a couple of dates afterwards. This had to be the same woman, and he would need an excuse to see her again to clear his mind. Laura Turner called about the time he was making that decision inviting him to a church function on Saturday.

"Hi Eric, it's Laura."

"Hey Laura, how are you today?" he asked half-heartedly.

"Fine. And how are you today?" she asked with an air of expectation.

"I'm good. Little slow here at the bank today, but there's always something to tend to."

"I bet. Look, I'm calling to invite you to the church's annual fundraiser for Skeet's Homeless Shelter over on Midway. It'll be lots of fun with prizes, games, and kids running all over the place. I'm one of the chaperones and I could use another set of eyes to watch over things. It starts about eight and we wrap up about noon," she says to him.

"Sounds great. I'm available Saturday so sure, I'll be glad to help out," he says to her.

"That's great. Thank you so much Eric. I'll see you then. Take care."

"Okay Laura, sure, I'll be there."

*

Minnie Hawkins was seventy-two years old and had been in the nursing home for three months when Audrey was released from prison. She had fallen down in the kitchen and cracked her pelvis but was able to call 911 using her mobile phone. The EMS arrived at her house within twenty minutes and came right in as the front door was unlocked. They were able to assess her injury, check vitals, and secure her for the ride to the hospital's emergency room. This was not her first hospital admission, so a relative and neighbor's contact information was on file. Her nephew Robert was called, and he was there within an hour.

*

Audrey entered the house, set down her belongings and looked around the spacious living room. There was a quiet stillness to the furnishings and not much had been changed in fifteen years. As she slowly walked about she took note to how clean and orderly the place was; the housekeeper had continued to come by once a month while Minnie was away. Audrey went into the bedroom she would inhabit, saw that it was well apportioned and used the land line to call Robert. He would come by, and they could go visit the facility where Minnie was in rehabilitation. He would give her an update on her Minnie's health, and the ground rules for Audrey to stay at the house.

CHAPTER THREE

Moving is a traumatic experience period. One moment you're here, then in an instant, seems like, you're there. Thus Audrey was having a sense of displacement, almost waiting for someone, or something to choreograph her next circumstance: Chow Time! Count Time! Medical Call! Mail Call! She was frozen standing in the kitchen marveling at what had transpired the past fifteen years and eight days. She was a convicted killer, she was a single female, and she was now expected to return to society and live a good and decent life. Sure she thought, I've lived with liars, thieves, and unbred persons for most of my life and now I'm supposed to be decent!? Reality is she had become a decent person, she had put together a disciplined, rightful existence in Cell Block "C" for years now, staying out of trouble, following most of the rules, and walking away from disturbed individuals, both with name tags and numbers on their shirts. She had been a model prisoner, so unlike the wild child who entered Fulton County Corrections that July 1998. The one they called 'crazy girl' who cursed, and mocked, and generally didn't want to live. She was a far cry from the unkempt, smelly, and foul person she was then. She could be looked upon as being someone's partner.

*

Cousin Robert was four years older and had largely forgotten the details of Audrey's younger self. He had been a good student, involved in school events, went off to college, got married, and lived far removed from what she had experienced. He remembered Horace, Minnie's husband, talking about having to get her out of jail a couple of times and having a talk with a man who assaulted her in public once, so generally he didn't know much about her otherwise. Their communications the past two months had been positive, and he felt good about her moving back to Thomaston and benefitting from her inheritance. He was looking forward to meeting her in person.

*

Floyd Lawson was twenty-five, employed, yet still living at home with his parents before he met Audrey. He was a good guy, worked for the phone company, had a nice car, and had stopped taking drugs and drinking alcohol a year earlier. He had gone out for a sub sandwich one evening and she was standing in front of the store hustling for dollars. She spoke to him, and he spoke back but went on in to order his food. When he walked out ten minutes later she was still there and asked if he needed any drugs. He said no but had a physical reaction to her seductive voice and movements. He hesitated a moment and asked her, "What kind?"

"The good stuff," she replied.

He knew he was about to make a big mistake, but he asked her name. She told him and a conversation started. He motioned to his car, and they rode off. The next morning he was found in his car on Route 25 dead from a heroin overdose. People from the sub shop remembered he had picked up the young woman last night about six, and the police found and questioned her near Harvey's liquor store two days later. She was charged with his death. Coincidentally, Eric Gaines had a date with her six weeks prior.

CHAPTER FOUR

Lawrence Peterson was not a bad man, but he had issues. He was not the sharpest pencil in the cup, but he tried to provide a good home for himself and Audrey which became harder when Sheila, his wife of eight years walked off with another man and never returned. Audrey was six and a half years old at the time.

Larry, as he was called, worked for Motors Automotive ten hours a day and Audrey would go to Aunt Minnie and Horace's house after school, and he would pick her up around seven. They would feed her, play games, and generally support the needs of the youngster. Audrey was an active, inquisitive child and they were very patient and nurturing with her.

Audrey was always glad to see her daddy when he arrived, rushing up to him for a hug and the big smile he would give her. He loved his daughter and hoped she would not miss her mother too much, as Sheila had been adequate in every way, mostly; she just became addicted to alcohol and slowly relinquished her duties as a mother when Audrey started Kindergarten. Minnie stepped in and it was at her house that they had the talk with Audrey about her mother's leaving. They sat in the living room playing an old-fashioned math game of speed drills where each would have a sequence of numbers to add, subtract, multiply, or divide which was a lot of fun. Audrey remembered playing it with her mother and father and asked about Sheila.

"Daddy, when is momma coming back to play with us?" she asked a few moments into the night's game.

Minnie looked at Lawrence as she knew her brother wanted her to answer the question first, and then he would add on to her reply.

"Honey, your daddy has worked hard all day, let's just play the game and he'll talk about that when he feels better," Minnie replied to the girl.

"But daddy, she should be back by now. I miss her. When is she coming back?"

"Darling," he began, "I guess now is the time to tell you." He looks around the room, pauses a few more seconds, then starts:

"You may not understand what I'm about to say, but we're going to try to tell you in an honest way."

"Daddy, I know some things."

"Good darling. Okay, she's not coming back. She had somewhere else she wanted to be. She still loves you, but she had to go somewhere else."

"You mean like another job?" she asks earnestly.

"Yeah, another job, yeah, like another job."

"Will I be able to see her at that other job?"

"I don't think so darling, she can't have visitors."

Minnie, detecting the toll this was taking on Lawrence stepped in.

"Audrey, your father, me, and Horace love you very much, and we will take care of you. What do you remember about your mother?"

"I remember she was home then she would not be home much. She should be home, like all mommies."

"I know dear, but sometimes things change."

"Is daddy going to go too and leave me with you?" she asks her aunt.

"No, he's not going to leave you. He'll be with you forever."

"Okay, that's good," Audrey says and returns to the game.

*

Thomaston was a coastal town of about 16,000 residents and its county seat, Dublin, had the largest disparity of wealth in the state. There were two paper mills, shipping docks, shrimpers, and all sorts of containers moving in and out of its port. The downtown area was reviving as artisans, restauranteurs, and commercial ventures sought out the area now. The middle class was stable, and a brisk tourist trade for the nearby islands kept things humming year 'round. Lawrence and

Sheila moved here from Atlanta back in 1976 seeking a slower and less complicated lifestyle. She was an assistant office manager, and he worked for a large auto dealership as a mechanic. They made enough money to support their modest lifestyle. Trouble began when Lawrence stopped smoking weed and drinking alcohol to excess. Sheila tried to stop on several occasions, and did stay sober while carrying Audrey to term, but gradually started back, with some control for a few years. She worked for a time at the T-Shirt Factory and would come home later and later as time went on. When Audrey was about four there were two incidents where she was found with men who drank alcohol the way she did and eventually she had an affair with Charles Moore. A year or so later she packed her bags and left town. They have not heard from or seen her since.

CHAPTER FIVE

Robert called and told Audrey he would come by the house about three o'clock. She said that was fine. She had taken a restful nap for about an hour and that would give her time to freshen up. She also mentioned to him that she had not eaten and asked if they could stop on the way to the facility and get something to eat. He replied that he would go her one better and have his wife put together a plate of their last night's leftovers and she could eat a home cooked meal before they head out. She thanked him and looked forward to that.

She had walked about the house, looking at family pictures, testing furniture, and generally appreciating the fact that this would be her new home; kitchen appliances were up to date, exterior landscaping was fine, and the views up and down the street lent themselves to a sense of community as yards were well maintained, and the houses spaced comfortably. There were palm trees in front of most properties, and the live oaks were abundant, with the Spanish moss hanging prominently. Though she had grown up here it was all very new to her, cement blocks, metal doors with reinforced glass, and plastic ware had been the norm for the past fifteen years.

State prisons are tough places. The population is younger and poorer than federal. There's always a question of who controls what and how long you're in for. Like Audrey, when she first entered the system, inmates are usually wild and boisterous, poorly behaved, and not well adjusted to whatever good they had known. You didn't hear much talk of improving ones status in life, it's the anger and frustration of bad breaks and bad choices, of being low-level criminals used to sub-par living with not much prospect for social mobility, as it were. Where you landed was where you stayed.

Audrey was more fortunate than most. After the first few years of proving she was bad and a survivor she could look to better days ahead. She stayed sober, took classes, separated herself from the never-do-wells, and began to mature as a young woman. She had a small clerical job to go to each day for a few hours and encouraged her cellmate to maintain a positive living arrangement.

*

Robert arrived promptly at three taking pains to keep the food level and secure in his hands. He quickly walked the side pathway from the driveway and pushed the doorbell to alert Audrey of his arrival. She was at the back of the house lost in thoughts about their finally meeting again after all these years.

Robert was tall, lean, and handsome, not much wear of the world shone on his face or movements. He was business like and generally spent more time inside than out at home or his office downtown, but he had a rigorous physical regimen that included jogging and occasional hoops with old friends in the gym. He took note that the landscapers had removed the dead bush from in front of the porch and that the summer growth had been pruned just enough to allow for the understated beauty of the green, yellow, and purple flowers to show forth.

Audrey answered the door as if she were the madame of the house and appeared much taller than what Robert remembered. She had been so thin and withered the last time he saw her. She smiled graciously and asked him to come in. He did not think she was acting ahead of herself and was glad to see a confident woman who seemed ready for the challenges ahead.

"Hey Robert," she blurted out, anxious to talk to someone again.

"Audrey, you look great," he says to her, entering the house and heading for the kitchen.

"Smells good," she says following him as he briskly moves past her.

"Yes, I think you'll enjoy it."

"I'm ready!"

He places the two dishes on the oval shaped table with the blue and white checker cloth evenly spread out, removes the aluminum foil, and shows off the plates of Meatloaf, mashed potatoes, collard greens, cornbread, and a dish of peach cobbler: enough portions for two meals.

"Wow, this is great! Yum, Yum," Audrey exclaims, licking her lips, and looking around for the drawer that holds the eating utensils. She finds it directly behind her and takes out a fork, spoon, and a knife.

Robert gestures for her to sit, reaches in a cabinet to get another plate out and begins to apportion a decent size meal for her to start with, and places it in the microwave oven for one minute.

"Robert, this is great. I really appreciate it."

"My pleasure. Take your time, eat, enjoy. Would you like to eat alone first, or should I stay here, and we can talk?" he asks her, respecting the newness of it all.

"No, please, I'll eat slowly, though I'm ready to devour it all in one gulp!"

They share a gentle laugh.

*

Eric arrived early for the fundraiser and watched as Laura arranged booths and hung helium filled balloons at the four corners of the block. Some family members with kids were already taking advantage of the rides and refreshments and the screaming excitement of about six children running around the newly constructed sandbox filled the air. It was a festive atmosphere for a bright, summer morning already.

Laura waved and walked towards him after repositioning a table, smiling, and controlling her steps so as not to give away how anxious she was to see him. You couldn't say it was love but she really liked him.

"Hey cutie," she says, blushing and turning away from him quickly."

"You look pretty good yourself," he says to her.

"Thanks for coming early. Let me show you around and what I'd like for you to do mostly.

"Sure, I'm at your service."

CHAPTER SIX

"There is this haunting feeling about me, an over-awareness of my existence, a something that is with me, undefined yet powerful and exhausting, pushing me forward to where I don't know, a will, a force, an idea, a memory perhaps, dark, and isolated, present, yet far away."

Audrey was thinking this as she took the first few bites of food, seeming to disassociate from the moment with Robert, wondering if this were real, or a dream from prison or before, someone else's life, something that happened that produced a blackout, something horrible, or simply a survival, a witnessing, what was it?

"How is it?" he asked her, noticing the faraway stare.

"Oh it's great, I was starving; this is good. How about you, did you have lunch already?" she asks, chewing quickly.

"Sure, I had a big lunch with Kathy. I'll have this same dinner when I get home later."

"Good. I mean this is sohhh good!"

*

Robert's private assessment so far is that his cousin is genuine and honest. She seems changed, as it were. He doesn't have a sense of fear or that he's sitting with a criminal, whatever that means. It's his first cousin, family, and she, just like he has arrived at a certain stage of life determined by actions of a certain type over a long period of time.

"Aunt Minnie asked about you," he interjects into the conversation.

"Oh yeah, what's the story?" she asks.

"She was wondering how you were doing, how you looked."

"What'd you tell her?"

"I told her you looked good in the pictures you sent, and she would see for herself when we got there."

"It's mighty generous of her to let me stay at her house."

"Yes it is, but you did grow up here; how long was it?"

"Ten years or so, you know, I was a wild child the last few years. I'm sure that's not a pretty picture for her to remember."

"She doesn't remember much, and I guess now is the time to tell you, she won't be coming back here. Her situation is grave so it's good we're going to see her today," Robert shares.

"How bad?" Audrey asks him, seeming to miss the point.

"She'll be transferring to Hospice this week," he states directly.

"Wow, I didn't know it was that bad."

"Well, you've just arrived. We'll talk more on the ride over to Kenyon's Recovery Center, it's about twenty minutes away."

"Okay, good."

*

Minnie was able to sit up in bed today. The level of pain and discomfort of the past week had subsided, and she was enjoying the music her roommate played from her mobile phone most afternoons, particularly the Mozart Sonatas. She was looking forward to the visit of her niece and nephew but couldn't remember which one went to prison. She would have to ring for assistance if she wanted to walk around a bit before thy arrived, but she didn't, feeling content to sit and think about her past.

She thought of Horace, and the years they spent travelling around the country, particularly 2004 through 2011. Those were the Desert Years, when New Mexico and Arizona seemed to pull them back each Spring. She thought of growing up with her brother Lawrence and how he poked fun at her because she was a girl and couldn't run as fast as he could or fight the way he did. But he loved her, and they were the best of friends.

She did have a mixed emotional response however when she thought of his daughter and what he told her about their relationship before he died. A seven-year-old child should not have to take on adult responsibilities, but he had her rub his chest, vigorously, when the pains were intense, or the fact that she slept beside him most nights to give him the comfort of not being alone. Or the way she would have to dress and undress him each day, no, some of that was not right, but something disrupted his thinking to the point that what she did that last night was to stop him from hurting and screaming. It was not a premeditated act, some other force intervened so that they could be relieved of a burden. What needed to happen did. What she was able to do should have been above her abilities to perform, but it was necessary, and no one else knew what went on in that household except Minnie. Larry had been honest with her two days before he died.

*

Kenyon's Recovery Center was an old, established rehabilitation facility run by a group of medical professionals who cared about the elderly and infirm. They had good core values and hired the best of the best. Terrance Lawson was the CEO and was well respected in the community for what he had put together twenty-five years ago. It was a well-run operation, and Robert was pleased that the doctors had referred Minnie here to heal from her pelvic injury. It took about two weeks for her blood tests and x-rays to confirm that she had inoperable colon cancer as well and perhaps four months to live.

Kenyon's was set on forty-two acres of now prime real estate in the northeastern corner of Thomaston. It was a lush campus full of pine, maple, and white oak trees. The physical care, treatment, and office buildings were one level structures designed to give a sense of wholistic, clinical calm. There were ramps and walkways to facilitate push or electric wheelchairs, single leg braces that fit knees or ankles, patients with canes or crutches, no effort was spared to give optimum twenty-first century, state of the sciences mental and physical rehabilitation services. Dr. Kenneth Gardner was leaving the cavernous, long, residential suite of rooms when Robert and Audrey entered the building. Dr. Gardner recognized Robert and came over to speak to them.

"Mr. Hawkins, so good to see you. May I have a word?"

"Yes, Dr. Gardner, this is my cousin, Audrey."

"Yes, yes. Good to meet you," the doctor says, speaking directly to her, then looking back to Robert.

"She's not well, and it's good you're here to visit. I'll be back in two days and go over the clinicals with you. Staff should have transfer plans in place by then."

"Yes sir, thank you. See you then," Robert responds as the doctor moves on.

CHAPTER SEVEN

Eric was trying to warm up to the fact that Laura had plans for his life. She was nice, but he didn't feel crazy about her. They'd had a few dates, and he came recently to Bible Study when she asked him to attend, but his thoughts had been more towards Ms. Peterson and what happened with them many years ago. Those sparks were real for him, even though alcohol induced. He felt them again seeing her at the bank the other day and was sure he should pursue her.

*

Laura sensed a rather lackadaisical participation from Eric, even though he was helpful with the collection of donations and feeding the homeless who were invited from the shelter. He didn't give her much of a sense of connection, or that he wanted to spend much time with her. He smiled and was cordial to all as most of the townspeople who stopped by banked with Southern and had known him a long time. He was a welcoming, good person, but his attention was elsewhere, and Laura knew it.

As the proceedings wrapped up and Laura thanked him for helping she asked him to come over to her house for dinner and a movie later. He was surprised by the offer, though he should not have been, and said yes, he was available and would love to. Laura was excited and told him to stop by about six.

*

Walking through the reception area and turning right into the long and spacious main hallway at Kenyon's was an awe-inspiring experience, the total length was one eight of a mile. The walls were adorned with works of art of museum quality, mostly landscapes of pastoral settings, and were ten yards apart. The theme was space, peace, and serenity. About fifteen yards in, past the public restrooms, you entered the treatment area, sectioned off with posters of physical human forms clinically capturing the exact size of various body parts to better explain strategies used to address and repair injuries with clients. Turning left at the entrance you would pass administration offices, and the nurses station before encountering patient rooms further down the hallway and to the right. Millie's room was three doors past the nurses' station and had cautionary signs on the door, Fall, Memory, and Breathing Care.

Staff spoke to Robert in a familiar way as he had been a regular visitor the past two months and gave Audrey friendly smiles. She returned the gestures verbalizing hello at times.

"Mr. Hawkins how are you today?" a male nurse spoke, establishing eye contact from his seated position. "Ma'am," he nods towards Audrey.

"Hello Darius, this is Mrs. Hawkins' niece, my cousin of course, Audrey."

"Good to meet you, Audrey," he says rather blandly, distracted by his next assignment. "She's doing fine if you want to go on in."

"Thanks Darius," Robert says. They walk the few steps to room 306 and gently knock on the door before entering the room.

Minnie was dressed, not in a gown, but comfortable slacks and a stained blouse. She wore hospital issued ankle socks but wore her own house shoes. She smiled at the sight of Robert then focused on the woman with him.

"Hello Robert," she says slowly pronouncing each syllable. "Your wife looks different today."

"Oh Minnie, this is your niece, Audrey. You haven't seen her in a long time," he says to her.

"Is she a new wife?" Minnie asks, displaying her mental and hearing declines.

"No." Robert answers, but figures it best for them to sit, relax, and not throw too much at her at once. He moves some chairs around, borrowing one from Minnie's roommate who is asleep. Minnie remains on the side of her bed, focusing on Audrey.

"I know you," Minnie says as Audrey takes a seat near the foot of the bed. Robert had rolled his chair closer to her. "Who are your people?"

Robert was about to answer again but Audrey thought it time for her to speak. Minnie looked away, then back to Audrey confused by this stranger. There was a knock on the door as a gentleman from dietary was ready to bring in the evening meals. "Dietary!" he announced.

Minnie's eyes light up and she looks over to the doorway. Gary, who worked this unit in the evenings, strode in with a wide grin and spoke to Minnie first.

"Ms. Minnie, how are you doing this evening, got some good food for you?" he says looking to Audrey and Robert, then asking, "How y'all doing? This won't take but a second. Let's see, Ms. Minnie, let me pull your tray around here, sit back for me." She does and says "okay" softly. He places the covered plate on the rolling cart, gets it close to her, takes the lid off, then looks over to Tina, who's still asleep.

"Okay, she's asleep, I'm going to leave her food, and the nurse will probably have to come in and feed her," he says to no one in particular as he sets her plate on a cart near her bed, looks at her again, and walks out.

"That was a little odd," Audrey says to Robert.

"He's that way," Minnie says. "He's my friend. He's a busy man."

Minnie gathers her utensils and begins to eat, staying focused on Audrey.

"You're the one who went to prison," Minnie says after a time. "You had a good home, I know what happened to you though, pity, I know. But you should have done better. I love you; Robert loves you, your daddy..." she stops talking and looks away. Robert becomes uncomfortable but doesn't react. Audrey decides it's time to speak.

"Aunt Minnie, It's good to see you. I've thought of you often the last fifteen years while I was away. I'll always be grateful for you and Horace taking me in after daddy died. That was a big commitment, and I messed up there at the end. I became a drunk and a bad girl."

"You were a bad girl, all those men, you were too young. I couldn't help you," Minnie speaks.

Audrey sits back in her chair and looks over at Robert who doesn't quite know what to make of this last exchange or if he should say anything. Minnie continues eating, slowly chewing her food now, coughing at times, then she speaks again.

"Robert, when my niece comes home she should live at the house. She's a good girl, a woman by now. I don't know if she's married and has kids, but you help her. We raised her right; she lived with us for a long time. We raised her right but her daddy..."

"I will," Robert says.

Minnie stopped eating, pushed the food cart away from the bed, leaned back, swung her legs up on the bed, adjusted her position, and went to sleep. Robert and Audrey stayed for about ten minutes, talking over a few things, spoke to the charge nurse and aide who came in to check on Minnie, then left, saying they would return in a day or so.

*

Laura and Eric were having a good visit, having fun actually as Eric seemed genuinely happy and comfortable being with her this evening. He had arrived early and helped set the dinner table, and they each drank a glass of wine as conversation was light and entertaining; they shared stories from college and growing up experiences. Laura grew up in Darien, about ten miles east of Thomaston and they knew some of the same people by way of cross-county sports activities and dating habits, but they had never met until she moved here six years ago to teach first grade at the public elementary school. Eric worked in new accounts back then and she was one of his last customers before he finished his masters' degree and moved into the bank's real estate department.

After eating they cleaned up the dishes and started the movie she had selected. It was a nice romantic charmer with not too much tension or intrigue, so eventually they began to create some, touching and petting each other during the movie, getting closer as they sat on the sofa in the living room in front of the TV. Their actions became more suggestive, and they were kissing and disrobing in short order, not able to make it to the bedroom before extreme pleasure set in. They stroked and caressed each other there on the floor for a time not quite sure what just happened.

CHAPTER EIGHT

"What'd you think?" Robert asked Audrey as they drove away from Kenyon's.

"I'm not sure what to think. It was good to see her after all these years, yet her state of mind was chilling in one sense," Audrey says to him.

"Yeah, I'm kind of used to it, and I can't tell how far gone she is mentally, but we know she doesn't have long to live," he shares.

"Does she ever talk about my father in full sentences?"

"No. Notice how she mentioned him, then stopped."

"I did notice; that was curious. How about Horace?"

"There was a period a few months ago when she asked about him, the date of their wedding anniversary in particular, but that was short lived. He died six years ago."

"So where do I stand with all of this?"

"Well, as the will states the house is yours, and you've received the insurance funds that had been set aside for you. I guess it's time for you to live. The doctors say at the outside she has about two months. There is a car in the garage and that's yours as well. What are your plans?" he asks, trying to get a handle on her thinking thus far.

"Of course I should stay here and make a life for myself. It's beginning to feel like home, I guess, yet in a strange way. I was so messed up before," she shares, but stops short of remorse.

"That's the past. One step at a time. You're a new person with a new life. Don't look back much," he says searching to be kind and supportive.

"Seems like everything is in working order at the house so I just need to find a job and get started, right?"

"Take your time, I can give you a few leads. What skills do you have, or more specifically, what would you like to do?" he asks her.

"Clerical, customer service, I did that in prison; I want to be realistic even though I have a collection of short stories that I wrote while in prison. I'd like to sell them if I could."

"That's great. How do you plan to do that?"

"I don't know. It's nothing I have to deal with any time soon."

"That's true, but I would love to see them."

"Sure. They may not be great, but they represent a part of my life."

"We'll play around with it and see what happens. Get used to being here, move around, and we'll see. I've got some busy work to do the next few days, and I have to go back to the hospital day after tomorrow when Minnie is discharged to hospice. Oh, by the way Kathy says for you to call her and, she will be glad to ride around with you, go shopping of course, you know, she wants to help you get settled as well. And she's a reader too so mention your stories to her."

"That's good of you and your wife; I'll give her a call in the morning."

"That'd be fine."

"Okay, thank you Robert."

"Okay Audrey, have a good night."

*

It was a little after eight when Robert dropped Audrey off at the house. It had been a full day, and she was ready for a hot bath and some leisure time. She undressed, gathered two towels and face cloths from the closet and started her water. It was a wonderful sound to hear without the noise of other inmates jostling for time in the shower. She allowed the water to run hot, then cooled it a bit before stepping into the tub. She breathed a sigh of release and stood for a moment allowing the sensation of heat and gentle pressure on her feet and ankles to signal the start of a new chapter of life, free of the constant need to watch out for an angle or a threat disguised as a desire to be helpful, though that was a long time ago; her last five years inside were rather calm and free of strife.

She supported her weight and slowly eased into the water enjoying a sense of freedom and comfort she had dreamed about for so long. She splashed the warmth on her face and hair, relishing a sense of open cleanliness, a sense of wow about it all, a sense of being a somewhat hardened thirty-six years old woman, yet, with so much promise for a good life ahead. She heard the house phone ring and thought that maybe a friend of Minnie's was calling to check up on her. She hoped they would leave a message.

After her bath Audrey got into bed and slept for seven and a half hours.

CHAPTER NINE

It sounded like raindrops softly falling to rocks off the edge of the roof. She continued to listen and looked out the kitchen door window to the back porch. She noticed the line of pebbles going around this side of the house before seeing the kitten, a black and brown tabby about three months old huddled near the crate that held the boots and garden tools Minnie used. It was crying out for food and comfort.

She studied the scene wondering if a mother were near or some brothers and sisters as part of a litter and this one had only strayed a bit and would be rejoined with her family soon. After about five minutes Audrey went out the door for a closer look. The little one noticed her and meowed louder and stumbled in her direction. Audrey continued to survey the area and nothing else was moving or visible. She gingerly approached the small animal and made hushed, gentle sounds as she held out her hands in an open cup fashion. Kitty came closer and pushed her head to the fingertips and looked up to Audrey. Audrey began to cry as she blithely lifted her charge and snuggled it close to her chest. Perhaps she had met her first friend.

*

Minnie sat with thoughts of her brother, Lawrence, and the little girl who would grow up without her parents. She thought of the night before he died when she went to his house and listened as he talked of feeling alone and afraid, that he had become isolated from the world about him. He shared with her how he felt guilty for allowing the little girl to take care of him, relieving the pains in his chest and how he had her sleep in the same bed with him, how he needed the comfort, how he desperately needed the comfort she provided.

Minnie had listened, with some sense of alarm at what he might tell her, that he had crossed a boundary of some kind, that he had done something that would devastate the young child, that he had done an unforgivable. She interrupted once, fearing his confession would be too much for her to handle, but he held up a hand and asked to finish what he had to say.

"I know that it was wrong, that I should have asked you to come sooner, when the pain started, but she was so innocent and kind, wanting to help daddy, somehow knowing that I needed a wife, and that momma had disappeared, and that it was left up to her to be the woman of the house. She was too young to know that, yet willing to be of service. And no, I never touched her in an improper way, that she has not been soiled, only asked, rather allowed to comfort her father as a nurse would do. As one human being present for another."

*

Weeks passed and Eric had largely forgotten about Ms. Peterson; he and Laura were developing a comfortable relationship, and he was satisfied. Meanwhile, Audrey had taken the cat to the veterinarian's and had the usual tests and vaccinations performed. Leela was becoming quite the companion as she was steadier and healthier adjusting to her role as house pet. She had progressed from the old newspaper filled box to roaming each room of the house learning how to play and discharge in the appropriate places.

A Beginning!

OREO/A POEM

No, it is not cold out here because my heart is warm, and I am loved.

Yes, I am slower and have to rest, but I know you watch me as I prance through the meadow out by the lake, hunting, enjoying the open spaces.

Yes, I enjoy sitting on your pillow, waiting, not really paying attention to the birds that eat at your feeder, but I do listen for when you open the back door and leave a morsel of food there in the yard

for me.

No, I was not ready to leave this life, but it was time.

Yes, thank you family for all the love!

Also by George H. Clowers, Jr.

All That We Are After
The Moon Is My Confessor
The Case for Larry Fleming
I Wish to Hear the Autumn Wind
A Place, Then Nowhere
I Paint, He Writes: Life Together
Book II and Others
There Is This Place
Corrupted Lives: One Lost, One Restored
The Case for Larry Fleming: The Bonus Edition
Another Side of Town: The Complete Short Stories
A Seasoned Road
After We Left the Farm
Images, and the Power of Being: Thought and Quiet
Street Wars: Beginnings and Endings
The Writer's Playground: Short Stories

Watch for more at https://www.georgeclowers.com.

About the Author

Retired substance use disorder counselor.

Read more at https://www.georgeclowers.com.

Milton Keynes UK
Ingram Content Group UK Ltd.
UKHW041951291124
451915UK00001B/115

9 798224 036561